# THE
# HISTORY OF
# WHITE PEOPLE
# IN
# AMERICA

# THE
# HISTORY OF
# WHITE PEOPLE
# IN
# AMERICA

MARTIN MULL
AND
ALLEN RUCKER

A Perigee Book

Perigee Books
are published by
The Putnam Publishing Group
200 Madison Avenue
New York, NY 10016

Photograph on page 113 is by Bill Owens, and used with
permission. All other photographs are used with the permission
of Fossil Films and Photos.

Library of Congress Cataloging-in-Publication Data

Mull, Martin.
   The history of white people in America.

   Bibliography: p.
   1. United States—Social life and customs—
1971-      —Anecdotes, facetiae, satire, etc.
I. Rucker, Allen.   II. Title.
E169.02.M85   1985        973.9        85-12464
ISBN 0-399-51193-8

Printed in the United States of America
     2   3   4   5   6   7   8   9   10

# Acknowledgments

Briefly, we would like to thank the following people for their considerable aid and support in bringing this book about.

Charles Engel, Nancy Cushing-Jones, Gene Brissie, Ned Nalle, John Hornick, Janét Saunders, Peter Giagni, Ted Steinberg, Lauri Rodich, Pierce Rafferty, Bill Owens, and of course, the late Jinx Harrison.

If you don't like the book, remember, these people had something to do with it.

To our moms, and to our wives,
who are a lot like our moms,
only different.

# Contents

# PREFACE

Where does someone get an idea like a book on the history of White people in America? Do these ideas just float around in the air and drop on you when you least expect it, like those clam shells that pesky sea gulls drop on the roof of your rented summer house on Long Island when you're trying to get some sleep after playing squash all day with your brother-in-law? Perhaps, but not in this case.

It was earlier that evening. A chance get-together of family, college chums, and business associates led to a spirited discussion of ethnic origins. Things heated up quickly and soon even the caterers were chiming in.

My college roommate, Sid Sidberg, launched into a treatise on the Old Testament and had gotten through most of it when his cab finally arrived. My secretary, Barbara Romanoff, traced her family back to sixteenth-century Leningrad. An avid snowmobiler, she plans to go back there once "that Communist nuisance," as she put it, goes away. Our jaws all dropped as Anthony Jackson, the bartender, regaled us with hand-me-down ancestral stories of eating human flesh and boomerang-chucking techniques.

And so it went, one fascinating tale of ethnic pride

after another. And then, curse the darkness, it was my turn. I began to hyperventilate. It wasn't the fear of public speaking and it wasn't the Paul Masson wine that had me gasping in a paper bag. It was my essential rootlessness in a room full of well-rooted people. What was I? Where did I stem from? What did I remember? What could I say?

I said good night.

Feeling my considerable discomfort, all of my ethnically secure guests left quickly. There I was, alone in my Whiteness. "That's it!" I exclaimed, not too loudly. "I'm White! I'm a White person! A no-frills, middle-of-the-road, plain-as-the-nose-on-your-face White person!"

I ran to the door to tell my friends, but the bus had come and gone. No matter. I now knew my mission. What does it mean to be White in America? Does White simply mean "free of color" or "the color of new snow or milk," as *Webster's* defines it? Or is it a culture we can point to and be proud of?

I made it my business to find out. Hence, this book.

Cedar Rapids, 1985

12

I had the same idea at exactly the same time. I got it while filling out a census form. Under ethnic group, I put "Don't Know" and they told me to come up with something fast or they would count me as a Canadian.

Grand Rapids, 1985

Before we proceed, a note of caution. Every book that purports to include some people naturally excludes others. There's no reason to argue about it. It goes with the territory.

If you feel excluded from this study of White American life, it is probably because you don't have the slightest trace of Whiteness in your family tree or daily diet. But have no fear. Whatever *you* are is probably good, too. And since most White people would secretly like to be something else anyway, they probably want to be like you.

In any case, we hope no non-White feels offended by what is said here. We mean no harm. White people rarely mean to offend. In fact, they hate it. They are just so narrow-minded that they sometimes forget that there is anyone else out there.

# 1

## What Makes Us White?

Who exactly is White? And what makes them that way? Simply to be glib and cavalier and declare that anyone with White skin is White is a little too glib and cavalier. It is also misleading, downright incorrect, and potentially libelous.

It is in the interest of avoiding the latter, a long, drawn-out, costly libel suit, that we, the authors and our lawyers, feel more explanation is mandatory.

Let's start out in reverse and work forward from there. Let's be positive about what White people are not.

1. White people do not have a language of their own. They simply adopt the language of the country they are living in, usually English, adding to it a handful of catchphrases that allow them to identify themselves to each other. You could be in the middle of Kuwait and overhear a casual comment along the lines of "Darn it, Marge, my dogs are killing me. Let me take a load off here by the Buddha while you put on a new face," and you know you are in the company of Whites.

2. White people do not have a specific religion. They cover the spiritual parking lot from just south of Lutheran to due north of Christian Science. You won't find religious iconography on a White living room mantel or automobile dashboard. In a traditional White household, you may find a Bible, King James or Reader's Digest Condensed, but you won't find a bookmark in it. Possibly some autumn leaves or a pressed prom corsage, but no bookmark. To these folks, the Bible is more furniture than literature.

Not to say there isn't a reverence for the Almighty among Whites. There definitely is, and it usually manifests itself before the Sunday midday meal, in the form of grace. Every White, young and old, is ready with a rote blessing if called upon. If it's just the boys sitting around watching the ball game over BLTs, you're liable to hear, "Shall we say grace or just call her in?" followed by a hardy laugh and a somber "Amen." On more formal occasions, the head of the White household, usually the father, is often heard to recite the familiar and much-beloved pre-soup salutation, "Good food, good meat, good God, let's eat!"

3. White people do not have a recognizable style of dress, uniform, or folk costume. They dress like everyone else, or so it seems to them. Living mostly in temperate climates, they have never felt the need to design elaborate defenses against the ravages of Mother Nature, with the exception of golf and sailing apparel, of course. In short, you can't spot a White person by his garb alone, like you can spot a sumo wrestler, a hula dancer, or a rabbi. (The people at J. C. Penney's have long recognized this White dressing problem and have been doing something about it. For more on their unique and stylish Expand-A-Belt line of fine fashions, see Chapter Two.)

## WHITE ARTIFACTS

What Whites do have is artifacts, and tons of them. This is where we will begin our search for the White soul.

We do it with some trepidation. After all, you can't sum up a culture or a way of life by merely cataloging artifacts. It's too tricky. Anyone can either include or exclude himself from the group just by declaring, "Hey, we don't have one of those, I guess we're not one of them!" Or, "Hey, we do have one of those, I guess we're part of the club!" Or, for the social climber, "We need to get one of those," or more often than admitted, "Where can we rent one of those?" Of course, the rich White person will react, "Christ, didn't we just give four of those to the Goodwill?"

It is impossible to tell a great work of art by its frame. However, a truly great work of art generally has a pretty fancy frame, as well it should. Thus it gives the layman, who wouldn't know a great painting if it bit him on the inner thigh, a subtle but unmistakable hint that he is in the presence of something worth looking at, and should put out his cigarette and shut up except for a couple of reverent oohs and aahs.

In much the same way, the White artifact helps frame the White experience every step of the way. Let's face it, White people have a love for doodads and gizmos and time-savers and corner-cutters and affordable, easy-to-grasp objets d'art, big and small. You won't find a White household devoid of these things. We've looked all day and it's just not out there.

## The Humorous Doormat

Whites are a friendly, outgoing people and love to let you know that before you step into the house. Just look down at your feet and you know what you're in for. If the mat says, "It Takes a Heap of Livin' to Make a House a Home," you're liable to get smothered with kisses. If it's "God Bless Our Humble Abode," you know not to use the Lord's name in vain. A simple "Howdy, We're the Harrisons" probably means you won't get out of the house without a tuna sandwich or a handful of bridge mix.

19

*The Piggyback Washer/Dryer*

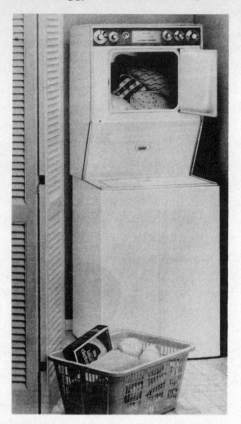

Let's take another salient example, this time in the appliance category: the piggyback combination washer and dryer. To many it's a luxury, to still others, an ephemeral dream that might one day grace their dirt floor, but to the White apartment dweller, it's a bone-marrow necessity of life. Why? For a number of reasons.

1. Other Whites have them and seem to like them, so why shouldn't we have one?
2. You can fit them into the hall closet and still have room for a folding card table, a set of wild-geese-motif TV trays, and a bag full of golf clubs.
3. If you close the closet door, you can't hear the darned thing whirring away during *Dynasty*.
4. Given their limited capacity, an average load (three pairs of nylons and a dish towel) can add up to a long and meaningful evening at home.
5. It beats the socks off of going down to Pepe's Laundro-de-Oro and getting your running togs all tangled up with someone else's serapes and loincloths and then having to learn the correct Armenian expression for "Change for a dollar, please." All laundromats make White people nervous. It's a fact.

### The Decorative Refrigerator Magnet

Let's move to another ubiquitous White trapping, albeit a smaller one: the decorative-mirth-provoking-magnetic-refrigerator-ornament. By itself, it's an instant attention grabber, icebreaker, and conversation starter—a bite-size ceramic pepperoni pizza; a fool-the-eye lifelike chocolate chip cookie; or a family of small enamel pigs proclaiming, "A moment on the lips, forever on the hips." But form follows function, and so do these little hold-'em-ups. Every one of them has a story to tell.

21

## Tales of Decorative Magnets

*TALE NUMBER 1*

Last night, Dr. Elmer Watson and the missus talked on and on about the rust spots on her ficus plant. She was beside herself with worry. What to do? The next morning, over his morning cup of coffee, Elmer spotted a whole article on the darn problem in the *Times*. Excited enough to wake her, but too considerate to do so, he did the next best thing. He carefully cut the item out of the paper, leaving ample margins, and secured it to the refrigerator with her favorite Happy Hippo magnet. He then headed off for work, knowing full well that when he called home later she would have seen it and read it several times, and that they could make plans to discuss it at length over dinner.

*TALE NUMBER 2*

Eight-year-old Billy Palmer is a good eater but a problem student. He has failed math, spelling, geography, everything that they throw at him. However, he has risen to at least household fame as, to quote his dad, "the first goddamn artist we ever had around this family, that's for sure." His artwork is an obvious source of pride around the Palmer home and is thus displayed prominently, where everyone can see it, on the freezer door of the family fridge. Check out his latest. It's a beaut. A beaut that may need some explaining.

The green thing in the corner is Billy's idea of a tree, and the squiggle under it is his dad, cutting it down with a chain saw. The red thing in the other corner is Billy's mom doing sit-ups. She's apparently on some kind of health kick. The four-inch-high letters in the middle are supposed to spell "Billy." You just have to imagine the other "L."

*TALE NUMBER 3*

Clara Beemish, like many 320-pound White women, lived alone in a modest apartment that was mostly kitchen. Her parents, Bob and Bertha, were also heavyweights and convinced Clara early in life that she could find the man of her dreams without losing an ounce. "If they can't handle your size, they're not man enough for you," Bob was fond of saying. "Just turn on that big smile of yours and let Cupid take care of the rest," her mother always chimed in.

Thirty-nine years later, Clara began to question this philosophy, as did her Aunt Josephine in St. Louis. Knowing Clara to be lonely and afraid of dying a spinster, Josephine sent her a clipping she had come across in a recent issue of *Family Circle*. It was the "Egg and Egg By-product Diet." Included in Aunt Jo's "care package" was the article itself, a gaily decorated calorie counter/menu planner, and two months' supply of the recommended egg by-product powder supplement. As per instructions, all the diet charts were strategically affixed to the refrigerator door. Clara, ever the home decorator with a gift for themes, found just the right quartet of magnets to secure them: a life-size fried egg, a rubber omelet, and a pair of adorable little fuzzy-wuzzy chickens.

Clara never expected the egg powder to be as tasty

and satisfying as her usual entrée, deep-dish pizza and a quart of Rocky Road, but it was there, and she ate it all in a single weekend. Only after her doctor diagnosed it as tainted with salmonella did she think twice about it, but by then she had been hospitalized for a month and lost 186 pounds.

And the good news didn't stop there. She met a male nurse who liked his women "with a little meat on their bones, but small enough to fit in bed." They got married in Reno soon after, and to this day, their marriage license is affixed to the fridge with, you guessed it, the same precious little magnets that started it all.

### Personalized Pencils

Another artifact: another story.

Dorothy and Dennis Cox forewent the option of having children to put virtually all of their time into their bowling alley, the Shangri-Lanes, a recreational experience that they summed up as "all the fun of bowling plus a South Seas setting." Obviously an idea *this* ground-breaking needed advertising. Simply having Dorothy dress in a Balinese sarong behind the bowling-shoes rental counter, as good an idea as it was, was not good enough. Sure it was jazzy. Sure it brought Dorothy a measure of personal recognition. But it didn't bring the repeat customers they so desperately needed. What could they do?

Because of their limited funds, a broad-based radio/TV campaign was immediately ruled out. But that didn't stop Dennis Cox. One evening while watching *Match Game PM* on television and leafing through his favorite mail-order catalog, he hit upon a gold mine of an idea that wouldn't cost him a gold mine: personalized "Welcome to Shangri-Lanes Country" complimentary pencils. Set of thirty, $4.69—enough for a month during the winter season, three months in the summer.

You can probably guess the rest. In a very short three and a half years, the Coxes were able to realize a lifelong dream: a 20-by-20-foot room addition to the lanes and, smack-dab in the middle, a brand-new Brunswick Bumper Pool Table with coin-operated ball return.

Personalized pencils—to most people a small White artifact of no consequence, but to Dennis Cox, it was "something I should have thought of years ago," and to his lovely wife Dorothy, it was "something Dennis should have thought of years ago."

### The Semipersonal Christmas Family Form Letter

This may be an obscure item to many of you, but in White America it is a seasonal experience as rich and constant as Perry Como's *Christmas in Belfast*. The idea is simple: Write one long letter telling everything you can think of that happened to you and yours in the past year, Xerox a hundred copies of it, and send them out to distant friends and relatives. You love sending it—it relieves a load of guilt about not keeping in touch. They love getting it—it's a lot meatier than something scribbled on the back of a

Hallmark card, and even if they don't know half of the people in the letter, it's fun to compare lives.

Here's one we came across:

Dear Everyone,

Well, it's getting to be that time again, so, as I've done for so many years, I went down in the basement to get out the old Royal (this year I finally bought a new ribbon!) and hauled it up to the den so I could let all of you know what the Armstrong clan has been up to since last Christmas. We're a pretty busy bunch. I hope I bought enough paper!!!!

Little Debby finally died. There's no sense dwelling on it, since the rest of the news is pretty good. Diane's wedding in the spring went off without a hitch—that's right, Julio never showed up, the heel. Sure, there were a few tears, mostly Diane's, but thanks to Bernice's catering and the church's open-bar policy in cases like this, it turned into a darn good time, even for Diane. She fell madly in love with Julio's best man, Ramone, who DID show up, and after they eloped later that evening, she confessed by phone that he was the father of her child all along, so it all worked out for the best.

Uncle Clyde finally hit the big time with his license plate collection. The Tri-County Art Association let him put it up down at the library for two whole weeks!!! It gave him something to do between 9 and 4:30 every day. He even got his picture in the paper, surrounded by his favorite out-of-state plates. Needless to say, there was no talking to "Mr. Famous" for about three weeks there.

Al wrote us from Germany. He sent along a lovely cuckoo clock for me and an ornamental beer stein for Dad. Apparently he's making the military a career. We still haven't seen a picture of his wife, but our guess is that she's blond, cute as a bug, and strong as an ox.

Not all the news is good. I'm still having loads of trouble with that drainage ditch out back. It must be the mosquito capital of the world. Chuck thinks we should stock it with bass. Apparently they love mosquitoes. He should know. He spent three years at college.

Gotta go now. Today's a big day—we're having the garage sale of Debby's things. Of course the hospital bed was rented and most of her clothes had to be burned, but everything else has a price tag on it. There's some real bargains out there. I think we'll do well. I'll let you know next Christmas.

Oops, I think I hear reindeer on the roof,

Love to all,
Your mother-grandmother-
                    sister-aunt-daughter-friend,

*Winnie*

27

PS. Roy, if you are still wrestling with that weight problem, here's a tip your dad sent on from Arizona: Expand-A-Belt trousers. As Dad says, "They grow with the flow." He got his at Penney's.

Needless to say, space does not permit a complete list of White artifacts and their accompanying stories. Suffice it to say that the clip-on bow tie is more than coincidentally related to the vaunted position of "Hardware Man of the Year." And the "Honk If You Love Jesus" license-plate holder serves a greater good than simply reducing plate rattle.

Thumb through any mail-order catalog and you will soon realize you are not looking at mere consumer items, you are looking at the secret lives of people, White people. A plastic picnic-table coverall ($7.98 postpaid) is not simply 12 yards of industrial strength polyurethane. It is a fun-loving family in the rainy Northwest. A piggy cracker-and-cookie cradle (10½ inches long, $13.98) is not just 39 cents' worth of ceramic clay on a green felt base. It is an understanding grandmother in Dubuque who realizes she has to spark up her get-togethers with a little humor, and small country touches add so much to today's entertaining and decorating themes. A spare toilet-paper holder that attaches right on the side of the bowl is a small White boy's way of saying "Happy Mother's Day, Mom."

We know what you're saying. "Hey, you don't need a White identity card to buy these things. Hell, a

Hindu can own a piggyback washer/dryer. What have you really proved?" You may not be saying this, but we are. We're more than aware that our argument here has more holes than a pegboard shop organizer ($13.95 at any hardware store), but we thought it made interesting reading and might prove valuable later on. This book is a long way from being over, so we don't know yet.

# 2

## Am I White?

The search for personal identity is as old as man, and maybe older. Most of us begin this search when we are eighteen, eighteen and a half, or nineteen, sitting around in a college dorm or army barracks, chatting with friends. But many of us, in the hubbub of daily life, never get around to such introspection, and when we die no one knows where to bury us or what to say at the funeral. If that's a potential problem for you, read on.

The following questionnaire was developed after years of intense research at the Institute for White Studies (IFWS), Zanesville, Ohio, under a grant from the J. C. Penney Company, Expand-A-Belt Division. It is intended for the private use of our readers and cannot be used or reproduced on job or home loan applications, résumés, civil service entrance exams, or census reports without the express written consent of the Institute. Furthermore, no question or answer should be construed to reflect directly on the effectiveness or durability of the Expand-A-Belt line of fine fashions.

This test should be administered only under optimum conditions. These include:

1. A quiet room, preferably a licensed Christian Science Reading Room. Or a study room at your local library if you don't believe that bunk about not going to a doctor when you're sick, as if a shot of penicillin spells the difference between Heaven and the Hot Place.
2. A No. 2 lead pencil, well sharpened. Mongol makes a good one. (Please initial all erasures.)

3. If you need a radio to help you think, keep it tuned to mild, middle-of-the-road music, no lyrics.
4. Upon completion, write at the bottom of your exam: "I have neither given nor received help on this paper." Sign your name, date it, and send, along with $106 (cash or money order—no checks, please), to:

Tell Me If I'm White or Not
THE INSTITUTE FOR WHITE STUDIES
Miracle Whip Square
Zanesville, Ohio 60605

You may now begin. You have fifteen minutes. Keep your own time.

1. Do you wear Expand-A-Belt trousers?
   _____ Always.
   _____ Only at home.
   _____ Wish I could.
   _____ Not available in my area.

2. Can you slam-dunk a basketball?
   _____ Yes.
   _____ No.
   _____ Could touch the rim in high school.

3. How many ways does Wonder bread help build strong bodies?
   _____ Eight.
   _____ More than eight.
   _____ At least eight.

4. How many neckties do you own? (Men only)
   _____ One.
   _____ One hundred.
   _____ Several hundred.

5. When a sultry, raven-haired Latin temptress in a low-cut sequined gown slinks up to you at the bar and asks for a light, you . . . (Men only)
   _____ Tell her she shouldn't smoke.
   _____ Shake hands and give her your business card.
   _____ Shout "Hoy-oh!" loudly, like Ed McMahon on *The Tonight Show*.

34

6. A great hamburger does not contain which of the following:

⎯⎯⎯⎯ Lipton's onion soup mix.

⎯⎯⎯⎯ Mayonnaise, and tons of it.

⎯⎯⎯⎯ Artificial grill marks.

⎯⎯⎯⎯ Jewish pickles.

7. The first thing you notice about another's home is:

⎯⎯⎯⎯ How it smells.

⎯⎯⎯⎯ Its resale value.

8. You are traveling to Europe on an expensive cruise ship. At seven in the morning there is a knock on your stateroom door and a man with a thick accent you can't pinpoint announces what sounds like breakfast. You . . .

⎯⎯⎯⎯ Make an attempt to learn his language.

⎯⎯⎯⎯ Insist that he learn yours.

⎯⎯⎯⎯ Tip him lavishly and bow, praying to God that it's the custom and he's really a waiter and not a terrorist.

9. A game of Scrabble becomes unbearable when:

⎯⎯⎯⎯ Your opponent won't stop talking about the storm-window business.

⎯⎯⎯⎯ Everybody leaves the room when it's your turn.

⎯⎯⎯⎯ There's no more Cheetos.

⎯⎯⎯⎯ Your Italian neighbor gets a triple on the word "goombahz" (with a "z").

35

10. The beauty of Expand-A-Belt trousers is:
_____ You don't need a belt.
_____ They stay up anyway.
_____ They are a perfect gift idea.
_____ They go great with the Expand-A-Jacket.

11. Your teenage daughter announces that she is a born-again Christian. There's a long silence, and then you:
_____ Jokingly ask what it cost, because the first time she was born set you back $600 and change.
_____ Tell her she's adopted.
_____ Go over your will with an eraser.
_____ Act like you didn't understand and say "Gesundheit."

12. How often do you check your breath?
_____ Upon reading this.
_____ When others wince.
_____ Once a year.

Take a breather. If these questions are tough for you, you probably aren't White and can go home now. Good night. If you're still not sure, keep working.

13. The world's most nearly perfect food is:
_____ Processed cheese.
_____ Stinky French cheese.
_____ Stinky German cheese.
_____ Donuts.

14. It's two days before Christmas. Your mail carrier, a non-White, announces that he's been fired from the post office, effective today, and that his wife is expecting triplets. He's provided excellent mail service for fourteen years, so you:

_____ Give him a lecture on birth control.

_____ Complain about all the junk mail you get.

_____ Tell him to wait while you go in the house and send your wife out with a check for one dollar.

15. A condominium is:

_____ Less than a home.

_____ A perfect home for your mother-in-law.

_____ Something that leaves a ring in your son's wallet.

16. You are waiting in your boss's car as he ducks into a 7-11 store for some Tums. The glove compartment inexplicably opens and out pops a large white bed sheet with two eyeholes and a hood. You:

_____ Ask if he's been sleeping in his car.

_____ Put it on as a joke and go into the 7-11 after him, yelling "Woogie, woogie, woogie!"

_____ Write a TV movie about your discovery.

17. You just bought a new car and that evening, you must hand it over to a Third World parking valet at your favorite restaurant. You:

_____ Ride with him as he parks it.

_____ Drive home and walk back to the restaurant.

_____ Empty the glove compartment into the trunk and give him only the ignition key.

_____ Eat at Denny's.

18. Upon hearing the oft-used phrase "Man's Best Friend," you immediately think of:

_____ Brut.

_____ A five iron.

_____ Bob Guccione.

_____ Expand-A-Belt trousers.

You're through. Push your paper away and take another breather. Better yet, stand up and stretch. It can't hurt. If it does hurt, sit down. No reason to kill yourself. It's just a harmless questionnaire, not an insurance physical.

If you are like any of the hundreds of people who have completed this exam, you are excited and confused. How did I do? Where do I stand? What's my score? Did I win?

First of all, the test was divided into four major areas. One, misleading or "trick" questions. Two, questions of no import whatsoever. Three, "gimmes," or questions only an idiot could get wrong. And four, questions required under a pre-existing contract with the fine folks at Expand-A-Belt fashions.

38

For example, question number 6, the one about hamburgers, was a dead giveaway. If you included "Jewish pickles" on your ideal burger, then give this book to a Methodist and go see *Yentl*. You'll learn a lot more about yourself than you will here. Suffice it to say that Barbra Streisand plays a young boy. That's all we're going to say. We don't want to spoil it for you.

Question number 7, however, was a trick question. If the first thing you notice about another's home is "how it smells," you were right. If the first thing you notice is "its resale value," you were also right. No matter what you answered, you were right, and well on your way to being White. Congratulations.

So you can see how it works. More than likely, you now have a strong inkling about yourself and your identity and are anxious to read more. And there's plenty more to read. So sit back, relax, unhinge those Expand-A-Belts, and follow us as we continue our journey through the history of White people in America.

# 3
## White Origins

Anyone who has plodded through Alex Haley's best-selling *Roots* knows the search for one's family origins can be a time-consuming, painstaking, yet often rewarding task.* Of course, Alex Haley had it easier than most. He could cut through a lot of meaningless singing groups and peanut farmers and head right for Africa.

As with everything else, the roots of White people are harder to pin down. It would be easy indeed to just assume that all White people came over on the *Mayflower* (above deck, as opposed to Alex's "crew"), but it's just not true. A few did, sure, but many more came over on more luxurious, privately owned cruise ships.

It has long been contended, especially by generations of White evangelists, that the first White people were created in the Garden of Eden. Historians, however, tell us that this mysterious garden must have been located right in downtown Israel. So much for Genesis.

Everyone has a theory, and it usually doesn't take more than a couple of cold Buds and some beer nuts to pull it out of them. To wit:

Recently a severe hailstorm and the subsequent flight delays brought us together with Waldo Bacon in the Layover Lounge at Kansas City International Airport. Waldo is sixty-seven years old, a retired

---

*Why would anyone, White or otherwise, waste his time reading a big, thick book when he can just watch the miniseries? Good point. However, we felt if we were going to write a book, we should read one first.

steam fitter, a veteran of "The Big One," and a born talker.

Here, in capsule form, is how Waldo perceives the origins of White people.

"Jinx and I spent hours, days, in that frigging foxhole, talking 'bout things. Jerry was no more than 200 some-odd yards away, so Jinx and I would have to talk soft. Boy, Jinx could talk your ear off, even soft. Of course, Jinx wasn't his real name. He picked that up while he was with the 101st Airborne. He'd pal around with a guy one day, the next day the guy'd be looking for his legs, so he started calling himself Jinx. It stuck.

"One night, when it was just raining bullets, Jinx said to me, 'Waldo, I'm scared, I'm scared shitless. If we ever get out of here alive, I'm getting rid of everything European I ever knew, ate, or did.' I said, 'Jinx, ol' buddy, I couldn't agree with you more. I think it's about time we had a culture all our own. I'm sick of Limeys, Krauts, Frogs, Wops, Porch-Geese, the whole lot of 'em. As soon as we get back, let's start from scratch.'

"Jinx nodded in agreement, lit a cigarette, and the next thing I knew I was in a V.A. hospital in Baltimore with the nickname 'Shorty.' I never knew what happened to Jinx."

That's one man's view. Here's another. Burt Tinker, of Tinker's Take-A-Trip travel agency in Allentown, Pennsylvania, maintains rather vocally that there are no White Americans, period. They don't exist, they never have. The whole lot of them are "simply transplanted Europeans who ought to go back every chance they can to see where they came from, if not for themselves, then, Chrissakes, for their kids." He further contends that you should "stay at least ten days, including one weekend, and book at least three months in advance, specifying smoking or nonsmoking, and arrange hotel, rent-a-cars, and wine-tasting tours through a reputable travel agent like me." Burt has plenty of brochures to back up his theory.

Rev. Rufus Jefferson, a venerable ninety-year-old gentleman of the cloth from Inkster, Michigan, dismisses all the foregoing with this simple statement: "White folk are just Black folk God didn't bother to finish."

We started to get frustrated. There seemed to be as many opinions as there were people to ask. We were forced into a position we had desperately hoped to avoid—go out and dig up information ourselves. We had to leave our typewriters by the pool and do some time-consuming legwork.

We walked down the block and zeroed in on a family we both had often considered to be just about the Whitest people we knew in the neighborhood. Last name: Harrison. First name: Hal. Wife's name: Joyce. Children: one each, Debby and Tommy.

Hal is an efficiency expert for a local supermarket chain. He loves his work and considers it important. "It shouldn't take longer to buy it than it does to eat it." In the late 1950s, as a young trainee, Hal helped pioneer the now widespread six-items-or-less express lane.

Joyce Harrison is a housewife and "darn proud of it—it's just like a real job, believe me." As demanding as homemaking can be, Joyce still finds time to run an Amway group, organize Tupperware parties, and head the steering committee for the local "Why Do You Think They Call It Dope?" antidrug campaign.

Debby Harrison, seventeen, is a cheerleader, straight-B student, with one eye on the boys and the other on college.

Tommy is a freckle-faced eleven-year-old who "still has plenty of time to bring his grades up." For the time being, skateboarding, ham radio, and acne do a better job of occupying his attention.

What struck us about the Harrison children is how much they looked up to their parents. We figured they must have gotten that from their parents themselves, who must have looked up to their parents, who must have looked up to their parents, right back to the first parents. What better White family tree could we find to climb?

The Harrisons readily agreed to tell us their family story, and we got the ball rolling one evening over a stack of family photo albums. There was history everywhere, in glowing black and white. Hal with his first car. Hal with his second car. Hal and Joyce with *their* first car. Hal and Joyce and baby Debby with the same car. And finally, the whole family, including the grandparents, standing in front of the same old car towing Hal's new boat. What an evening! First a short course in the history of the modern automobile, and then, pay dirt! We found ourselves staring at three generations of Harrisons in one grainy Ektachrome!

We pressed on and asked Hal and Joyce about their parents and their parents' parents. Hal took center stage while Joyce headed to the kitchen to brew up another pot of decaf and do the dishes.

"I didn't mean to chase Joyce out of here, but if it's the Harrisons you're interested in, you gotta talk to me. I'm the Harrison. She's a Miller. She's only a Harrison since I married her, which wasn't all that long ago, though sometimes it sure feels like it was, but that's not your problem, is it, fellas?" Joyce re-emerged with the steaming Sanka and Hal got back on track.

"Both of my parents were from Indiana, just outside of Fort Wayne. Mom was a Methodist, Dad was . . . well, as he put it, 'not really anything, but I know there's someone up there.' Dad sold vitrified sewer pipe and could have made a fortune if the war hadn't come along and taken both the pipe and him overseas. Dad must have been pretty popular over there because I can remember after he came back, we'd get these calls from ol' army buddies asking to talk to Jinx. That was a nickname he picked up over there. He never explained why.

"After Mom got hit by lightning in '58, Dad got out of the pipe business and moved up to Mount Saint Helens. He loves to fish. So do I. So does Tommy."

We decided to keep plunging back in time and arranged to meet with Jinx Harrison somewhere off the mountain. He liked Howard Johnson's, so did we. We taped the following interview over platters of fried clams.

*MM:* Well, Jinx, we know something about your past from your son, Hal.

46

*JH:* You don't know where I got the name Jinx, do you?

*MM:* Well, we've heard some stories.

*JH:* Well, don't believe them. Shorty's a liar.

*MM:* Mr. Harrison, what do you remember about your father, or, better yet, your grandfather?

*JH:* What makes you think my grandfather was better than my father?

*MM:* That's not what we're saying, it's just an expression.

*JH:* Oh . . . (*pause*) You gonna finish those?

*MM:* No, please, go ahead. I'm full.

*JH:* Great. Generally, I clean my plate and everyone else's. If I can't, I'll just take 'em home and pop 'em in the toaster oven for breakfast the next day, or scrape off the batter and use 'em for bait. Those crappies will eat anything.

*MM:* I'm sure they will, Mr. Harrison. Did your dad teach you about fishing?

*JH:* No, he hated to fish. He was a horseshoe man. Got him a ribbon once at the fair. You know, I got a lot of tartar sauce left over here. What's say we split another order of clams?

*MM:* Of course, Mr. Harrison, it's on us.

*AR:* I'll go see if they take MasterCharge.

*JH:* I don't think they do. Just Visa.

*MM:* Mr. Harrison, tell us, did your father ever tell you stories about his father, about the Civil War, for instance, and Lincoln freeing the slaves and writing incredible speeches on the back of envelopes, or maybe the settling of the West, White pioneers packing up wives and children

47

and all their worldly goods and striking out into a great unknown surrounded by scalp-crazed Indians and bad drinking water, or maybe the first time he saw an electric light or an iron horse chugging down the tracks, or maybe stories about his father's father's father and the Louisiana Purchase or the Declaration of Independence?

*JH:* No, he wasn't much of a talker.

*AR* (*nervously*): They only take cash.

*MM:* Shit, what are we gonna . . . (*fizz, click*).

At this point Jinx accidentally tripped our waitress, who in turn spilled a pot of boiling Postum all over our cassette recorder, thus terminating the interview.

Having run face first into the left field wall with the Harrison lineage we decide to ask Joyce Harrison (née Miller) about her back story.

We found Joyce to be charming, peppy, and a heck of a cupcake maker, but when it came time to plunge backward on our little time machine, she was really of no help at all. She did mention that the name Miller was a new addition to the family lexicon, having been changed from Meuller in 1939. As for the rest, she took a more spiritual stance.

"I think every day is a new beginning. There's no sense looking over your shoulder," says Joyce.

"Unless you're chasing a fly ball," adds hubby Hal, and we all have a good laugh, realizing that we've hit on an obvious White truth. Namely: "Why be bothered with history when you're secure enough to think you can make some?"

We finished our cupcakes and headed back to the pool.

# 4
## White Language

To say that the language of the White American is simply English is like saying that Mahatma Gandhi was just "a nice guy." The White American has taken the rudiments of English and used them as a spring-board, or "jumping-off place," as he himself would say, for developing a vocabulary that expresses his own uniqueness. Every group has an argot, a jargon, a set of code words, that they use to identify themselves to each other. It's just as preposterous for the White man to greet another with "Hey, bro, what's happenin'?" as it is for a Jewish tailor to say, "Howdy, bud, how're they treating ya?"

How many times have you, as a White, stood by in utter incomprehension while two teenage Black kids talked about whatever they were talking about. You might as well be on Mars. Perhaps that's why they put Nick Nolte in those Eddie Murphy movies, so you can at least follow half of the story.

Of course, to single out Black speech patterns as gibberish is unfair. White people tune out on *everyone* south of Kansas City and north of Connecticut. They can really only understand other people who talk "normal" like they do.

But isn't this how every ethnic group feels? Perhaps a conversation that Whites find plain, simple, and to the point is mumbo jumbo to others. In an attempt to make the White man better understood when confronting French waiters, valet parkers of all stripes, Japanese businessmen, maids, gardeners, and Armenian foreign-car specialists, we respectfully submit the following.

## A WHITE CONVERSATION

(The following conversation was secretly taped at the Tick-Tock Coffee Shop & Bakery, Hinton, Ohio. We chose the right place, wired the corner booth, and waited for the right people to show up. It didn't take long. The participants are Mrs. Irma Clark, a fifty-two-year-old taxidermist's assistant and mother; an old friend, Doris Fletcher; and later on, Doris's husband, Walt.)

*IRMA:* Oh, for crying out loud, look who's here!

*DORIS:* Well, for Pete's sake, it's been a coon's age, Irma.

*IRMA:* You're right, Doris, it's been a month of Sundays. Come on, take a load off.

*DORIS:* Don't mind if I do. Now, who do you have to know to get a cup of mud around here?

*IRMA:* Oh, the girl'll be right back. She's putting on a new face.

*DORIS:* My, Irma, you're looking bright as a new penny.

*IRMA:* You're a sight for sore eyes yourself.

*DORIS:* It takes one to know one.

*IRMA:* Ain't it the truth.

*DORIS:* So, are they keeping ya busy?

*IRMA:* Can't complain.

*DORIS:* That's the spirit. How's your better half?

*IRMA:* He's busy as a beaver. And yours?

*DORIS:* Speak of the devil. (*Up walks her husband, Walt.*)

51

WALT: Holy cow, Irma, we haven't seen you in a blue moon.

DORIS: Honey, I bet your ears were burning.

IRMA: Park it, Walt.

WALT: Speakin' of ears, I was just out gettin' mine lowered.

IRMA: Oh, you got a haircut.

WALT: Hell, I got 'em *all* cut! (*They all laugh.*)

IRMA: Heavens to Betsy, Walt, you're such a card!

WALT (*reaching for Irma's donut*): Listen, you plan to eat that thing or just worry it to death?

IRMA: Go ahead, I need it like a hole in the head. (*They sit silently, watching Walt eat the donut. The silence is broken by a waitress in the background.*)

WAITRESS (*yelling*): Pigs in a blanket, put legs on them, and a side of cow juice!

Now, as an experiment, let's take the same conversation and remove all the idiomatic White language.

IRMA: Hello, Doris.

DORIS: Hello, Irma.

WALT: I want to eat your donut.

WAITRESS (*in background*): Prepare two pancakes with sausage and a glass of milk, to go.

As you can see, this dialogue could have transpired in any ethnic group in any part of the world where they sell donuts and offer take-out service.

Obviously, to the White person, the use of familiar idiomatic expressions serves a purpose other than communicating ideas, should any occur. It provides the opportunity to "chat." Chatting is a uniquely White pastime. It fills the gaps in a White person's life, from the momentary gap between bids in a bridge game to the huge gap between birth and death. It relieves tension in a potentially hostile world. With chatting, a crowded elevator becomes a drinkless cocktail party, and a fearful New York cab ride becomes an interesting one-way conversation about how the Arabs are ruining everything.

If chatting can make the world a friendlier place, why doesn't everyone do it? Perhaps they don't know how. It's not as hard as it seems. To the White person, it's like falling out of bed, but everybody can learn to chat if they follow these few simple guidelines.

1. Don't be in a hurry.
2. Never express an opinion that hasn't been expressed on television, and bracket every opinion with "or so they say."
3. Pretend that you are interested in what the other person has to say.
4. When asked, "Have you heard this one?," always answer no.
5. Keep the conversation going, only stopping short at revealing anything about yourself or your feelings.
6. Acquire a taste for coffee.
7. Remember expressions that the other person uses so that you can use them yourself the next time you meet.

8. Don't argue.
9. Don't be afraid to repeat yourself.
10. When ending a chat, never say the word "good-bye." Any of the following are acceptable substitutions.
    a. "Don't be a stranger."
    b. "Keep in touch."
    c. "See you in the funny papers."
    d. "Don't let your meat loaf."
    e. "Don't do anything I wouldn't do, and if you do, name it after me."
    f. "Time to take my drum and beat it."
    g. "Guess I'll make like a horse turd and hit the trail."
    h. "I'm history."
    i. "Hasta lumbago, amigo." (Delivered with suitable accent.)

History shows us how words and phrases are created out of need. If a situation or substance occurs that is unique to the world, it is usually only a matter of moments before it has a name, NutraSweet being a recent example. From "Astroturf" to "zits," we are continually creating new additions to the language. Often the source of this creation is anger. For the White person this presents a problem.

White people hate to get angry, and hate even more to show it, much less voice it. However, in a fit of pique even White people are apt to come out with a stream of epithets or cuss words. Sometimes they don't even know they're doing it. How often have you heard a White man, once he's cooled down a bit, say,

"I didn't know what I was saying," or a White woman ask sincerely, "Did that come out of little old me?" If you, like thousands of White Americans, find yourself tongue-tied during moments of rage, perhaps the following glossary will prove helpful.

## WHITE SWEAR WORDS

### *For Women Only*

Mild anger. A situation that evokes this emotion might be the following:

The plastic spoon you use for the cat food falls into the Disposall and all of a sudden tomato seeds are blowing out of the drain all over your new kitchen curtains.

You might say:

1. "For crying out loud!"
2. "Oh, fudge!"
3. "Lord, why me?"

Now, for medium anger:

You're serving coffee to your mother-in-law and there are ants in the sugar.

1. "Oh, piddle poo!"
2. "Jesus H. Christ!"
3. "Lord grant me the wisdom to change the things that I can change, accept the things that I can't change, and to know the difference. Amen."

Now for the big stuff, a moment of fury:

Your husband was arrested in a police raid at Monique's House of Pleasure and the picture on the front page of the local paper shows him standing shirtless with two 300-pound Samoan women.

1. "Jiminy Christmas!"
2. "Shoot, shoot, and more shoot!"
3. "That lard ass, I'm gonna cut it off when he gets home!"

## For Men Only

Again, a situation provoking mild anger or distress:
Your daughter comes home from school minus her $3000 set of removable braces, stating she couldn't stand them anymore and threw them away.

1. "Rats!"
2. "Why, I oughta . . ."
3. "You make me so blinkety-blank mad!"

Medium anger:
A tornado hits your neighborhood, missing every house but yours.

1. "That does it, we're switching churches!"
2. "First the braces, now this!"
3. "Aetna, I'm glad I met ya!"

Now, unbridled rage:
You have just four-putted the thirteenth hole after hitting the green in one.

1. "Dog doo!"
2. "No, fellas, I had three putts, I swear to God!"
3. "This is the last fuckin' time I'm playing fuckin' golf with you fuckin' assholes on this fuckin' course until they fix the fuckin' greens! Give me a fuckin' beer, for Christ fuckin' sake!"

Well, enough of the swearing. It's a subject that makes a White person uncomfortable even to write about. Let's jump to something a little more pleasant, a higher plane, an area of language that White people heartily embrace: the concept of "Words to Live By." You'll find them everywhere in a White household. On decorative plates and party aprons. On bookmarks, matches, embroidered throw pillows, the cover of Mom's address book, and the bumper of Dad's camper. Many are available commercially in the form of lacquered plaques from Stuckey's, which can add "a woodsy wisdom" to even the smallest pine-paneled den.

We've saved the best until last. It is the marriage of the "Words to Live By" concept with the fine art of poetry. Sounds expensive, doesn't it? It's not. These gems can be found in thousands of greeting cards exchanged by millions of White Americans every year. Here's a sampling.

- The cover of this one shows a sad-eyed cocker spaniel and under it, the words "And So You've Lost Your Job Again."

*Dear Dad, you've brought us so much enjoyment,*

*Who cares if our dinner's "left over"?*

*We'll have meat and potatoes when you find employment,*

*'Til then we'll be sharing with Rover.*

• A cartoon bride and groom, handcuffed together, beam out at us from a sea of cartoon salt shakers and toasters. Under this it says, "You Finally Did It!"

*Our little girls found her Mr. Right,*

*We're happy as we can be.*

*And maybe we'll have a grandchild soon,*

*Who cares if it's nine months or three?*

• Against a purple backdrop, a picture of a man's shoe filled with flowers; beneath it, in fancy script, "On the Loss of Your Leg."

*You can be anything you think you can be,*

*As long as you're not thinking dancer.*

*You're young and you're White in a country that's free,*

*Let's just hope they got all the cancer.*

Since neither of us are poets, we'd be foolish to try and top these professional efforts. We just hope that we've given you a reasonable picture of Whitespeak and perhaps some new phrases to use the next time the "cat's got your tongue." Enough said.

# 5

## White Sex

To many, the title of this chapter is an anomaly, a contradiction in terms, like "towering miniseries" or *Bob Hope Special*. Be mindful of the fact that White people are still around in ever increasing numbers and these little White folk aren't crawling out from under a cabbage leaf. These babies are made by one means only. It's a scientific fact: Daddy has to put his thing in Mommy.

Long before the actual "doing it" occurs, a long, involved series of carefully executed rituals must transpire. Call it courtship, call it dating, call it trying to get laid, it still comes down to an intricate set of principles and practices tacitly understood by young White people everywhere.

To help us grasp these arcane rites of sexual initiation, let's trace a typical White courtship. Everyone, say hello to Bob and Cathy.

Bob and Cathy Nelson are a happily married White couple with a brand-new bouncing baby girl named Tracy. Bob and Cathy are both twenty-seven years old, but their courtship began when they were much younger.

Friday nights in Waterville were special nights for the kids at Bob Feller Junior High School. That was Teen-Canteen night. These brightly lit sock hops were jointly sponsored by the League of Women Voters and the Fire Department and offered the youngsters a chance to meet and mingle with the opposite sex. Mostly it meant the boys standing in one corner and talking about sports while they watched the girls fast-dance together. Then, about five of ten, the fire chief would lower the lights to three-quarters and announce the last dance, a ladies' choice. One Friday night, Cathy chose Bob after much prodding by her girl friends, and a reluctant Bob suddenly found himself actually feeling her bra strap through her angora sweater. As they danced even closer, he could feel the hooks as well. For Bob and Cathy there was no turning back.

Senior high came shortly and with it the "Passport to Pleasure": the driver's license. Since Cathy had to be in by eleven on weekends, and nine thirty on school nights, Bob had to plan their rendezvous with drill-team precision. Every outing had to be timed to allow for at least an hour and a half of "parking" down by Waterville's reservoir and sewage treatment plant.

During their junior year these countless hours added up to a lot of wrestling and passionate necking, culminating with Cathy's first French kiss. "I thought Bob threw up!!" she later said of the experience.

Then senior year came and with it an added maturity for Bob and Cathy. The door to more adult sexual expression was opened and, with it, a set of stringent rules.

1. Yes, you can unhook it and push it out of the way, but you can only touch them through my sweater.
2. You can't kiss them even through my sweater 'cause it will get my sweater wet and my dad will know.
3. If you want me to touch yours, you have to wear at least two pairs of clean underwear and keep them on.

4. You can only stick your hand down my panties in the back or on the side.
5. The radio has to be on at all times, and any time a Paul McCartney song comes on, you have to stop, because he's the cutest.
6. If you ever tell Frank Simmons what goes on in this car, I'll deny it and you'll never see me again.

Frank Simmons was the star quarterback for the Waterville High School football team. Six feet two and 190 pounds, Frank was virtually the whole team and a candidate for All-State honors. Frank could run, pass, kick, and block with the best of them. Bob, on the other hand, was more of a specialist. He was the placekick holder for Frank.

As head cheerleader, Cathy rooted for Frank and Bob equally on that fateful November afternoon showdown with Joe Louis Vocational. Frank was having the game of his life against a much superior opponent (half of the guys at Joe Louis were well into their twenties), but after three and a half quarters the game was still deadlocked at twenty-one all.

A mud-splattered field and a fractured fibula put the kibosh on Frank's personal running game, but his pinpoint passing led the intrepid Gamecocks to the Joe Louis four yard line with twelve seconds remaining to play.

Bob, in his spotless uniform, could almost hear his number being called as he paced the sidelines well within Cathy's gaze.

Rather than trying to re-create the exciting finale, let's go to a transcript of the original Waterville radio broadcast of the game. The announcer is local veterinarian Buzzy Braun, with color commentary by Bif Plymouth, Waterville's metal shop teacher.

*BUZZY:* That's the last time out for Waterville, Bif. . . .

*BIF:* And I have to add, Buzzy, it looks like curtains for Joe Louis. It's an easy kick for Simmons, broken leg or no broken leg. I've seen him make these suckers from forty, fifty yards out. This is a chip shot for Simmons, and another trophy for the Waterville display case, which was made by my shop class, I might add. . . .

*BUZZY:* Yep, Simmons is going to kick the three-pointer. Gardner, who's been in there the whole day, is going to snap it, no problem there. . . .

*BIF:* I'm a little worried about the holder, what's his name now. . . .

*BUZZY:* I'm looking it up—it's Nelson, Bob Nelson.

*BIF:* Actually, Buzzy, I doubt if there's anything to worry about. It's Nelson's last game as a senior. He won't let us down.

*BUZZY:* Well, they've broken out of the huddle and, as we guessed, it will be a field goal attempt by Simmons with twelve seconds to go. It couldn't get more exciting than this. Listen to that crowd.

*BIF:* Buzzy, I think you'd have to call it a "gimme." Some Joe Louis fans are already leaving.

BUZZY: Well, here we go. The snap is perfect. Nelson, the holder, lunges for the ball, slips, oh my God, the ball bounces off Nelson's helmet and straight up into the air into the Joe Louis secondary. And ... Jackson's got it and he's put on the afterburner, heading right for the Waterville goal.

BIF (*excitedly*): But Simmons is after him and is sure to catch him. . . .

BUZZY: Wait a minute, someone has stopped Simmons in his tracks, it's Nelson, the holder. He appears to be apologizing.

BIF: Well, he's got a lot more apologizing to do now, Buzzy. Jackson's just crossed the goal line, and there's the gun. Joe Louis wins it.

BUZZY: Boy, I wouldn't want to be Bob Nelson right now.

BIF: What an asshole.

Rather than face his hostile teammates in the Waterville dressing room, Bob elected to change out of his uniform in his car and then meet up with Cathy. The Victory Dance was of course canceled, so Bob and Cathy simply drove out to their parking spot at the reservoir in silence. Cathy had never seen Bob cry before, certainly not for two and a half hours straight. She tried kissing and stroking him, to no avail. Bob simply pushed her aside, continuing to mutter, "I can't believe I did it. I just can't believe it."

It was already ten thirty at night and time was running out. Cathy was at her wits' end. Then she accidentally stumbled on the right thing to say. "Bob, is there anything I can do to make you feel better? I'll do anything."

At eight thirty the next morning, two sewage treatment workers came upon the sleeping couple in the backseat of Bob's Camaro. "Hey, in there! Get some clothes on. We got sewage to treat!" said one of them. "I can't wait to tell Frank Simmons about this," said the other. Fortunately, for Bob, the sewage worker who made the second statement had an IQ that could be expressed on the fingers of one hand and he never remembered to tell Frank Simmons. So, for the rest of their senior year, Bob and Cathy enjoyed the secrecy of their lovemaking while continuing to practice and improve on it.

Despite what may seem like a blissful bound over the final hurdle into full sexual relations, there still were several rules and regulations that the young couple adhered to.

1. Not all the way in.
2. Pull out if you only even *think* you're going to "you know what."
3. Don't get any "you know what stuff" on my clothes.
4. If you ever tell Danny Clark about this, I'll deny it and you'll never see me again.

Danny Clark and Cathy were coeditors of the school paper, the *Watervillian,* and both had received handsome scholarships to Dayton University. Cathy obviously was concerned about keeping her reputation untarnished in the eyes of her fellow collegians.

67

Bob had hoped in vain for an athletic scholarship as a placekick holder. He found himself, instead, settling in as a full-tuition student at his father's alma mater, a small agricultural and mining school in Kentucky known simply as Pitman.

During their first year of college, Bob and Cathy wrote each other tireless letters and ran up enormous phone bills, which their parents paid for. This was not, as Bob's father often contended, "pissing away my paycheck." It was a crucial step in Bob and Cathy's emotional growth.

*OPERATOR:* That's three dollars for three minutes, please. (*CLANG, CLANG, CLANG, CLANG, CLANG, CLANG, CLANG, CLANG, CLANG, CLANG, CLANG.*) One more quarter, please.

*BOB:* Here's two dimes and . . . a nickel.

*OPERATOR:* Good enough. (*DING, DING, DONG.*)

*FEMALE VOICE:* Gamma House. Pledge Fredericks speaking.

*BOB:* Hi, Maureen, it's Bob Nelson, can I talk to Cathy, please.

*MAUREEN:* It's three o'clock in the morning, Bob, she's sleeping, for Chrissakes.

*BOB:* Well, tell her it's real important.

*MAUREEN* (*hollering down the hall*): Hey, Cathy, "Poopsie" is on the friggin' phone again!

68

CATHY (*picking up*): Bob, it's three o'clock in the morning, and I just talked to you an hour ago. What's so damned important?

BOB: Cathy, are you wearing my pin?

CATHY: Right now? I'm in my nightie!

BOB: No, I mean, every day, to class and stuff.

CATHY: Is that why you called?

BOB: Well, yeah, it's real important to me.

CATHY (*yawning*): Yeah, I wear it every day, Bob, right on my sweater next to my heart.

BOB: How close to your breast?

CATHY: Well, there's one on either side of my heart, Poopsie. Why?

BOB: Cuz, I don't want you to wear it right on your breast, because guys could come up and say, "Let me see your pin," and you know what they're really looking at and I don't like that and that's why I called.

CATHY: Bob, that's sweet. Tomorrow, I'll be sure to pin it on my collar right up by my neck. But right now, as I said, I'm in my nightie and I don't want to scratch myself.

BOB: What do you have on underneath?

CATHY: I don't want to go into it, Bob, you'll just get excited and anyway

I've got a seven thirty Psych class
tomorrow.

*BOB:* Okay. I'll call you about seven fifteen.

*CATHY:* I know you will, Poopsie.

*BOB:* Good night, Poopsie. (*click*)

Whenever possible Bob would rev up the now famous Camaro and drive the 600 some-odd miles from
Pitman to Dayton. The excuse would vary: a football
game; a mixer; a homecoming dance. The result was
always the same. It was a chance to get a booster shot
of their "semipenetration" sex life.

Cathy seemed absolutely satisfied with this rela-
tionship and remained true to Bob. Bob feigned satis-
faction with a blithe exterior. As he often said to
Cathy, "Hey, c'mon! It's better than nothing." But
was it? In his senior year Bob fell victim to a situation
all too familiar to many young White boys. And it was
all Elmo Stannard's fault.

Elmo was Bob's roommate from day one at Pitman.
Whereas Bob seemed to have little difficulty main-
taining a C average, Elmo, despite a relatively easy
Harvesting and Planting Techniques major, found
himself, after three years of struggling, on the dean's
"other" list. Expulsion for Elmo was imminent.

Elmo saw the writing on the wall and one evening
shortly thereafter announced to Bob and his other
frat brothers at the Alpha Beta House that he had
joined the army, effective tomorrow, and that a little
celebration was in order. Stunned, and eager to
party, Bob and the others agreed.

White college boys have a unique sense of fun. Gen-

erally a "fun" evening will go through several distinct
stages. First, the participants in the fun spend a good
deal of time by themselves getting shitfaced enough
to invite other participants; usually this means
women. Depending on the extent of the "shitface-
itude," these women will be either unsuspecting sorority girls from a nearby campus or "professional"
women. Elmo was adamant about not spending his
last civilian night with sorority girls.

Bob, like all young White men, had often and
loudly proclaimed his sexual prowess, so, when Elmo
drunkenly declared his plan for all of the brothers to
visit the local lady of ill repute, Bob was helpless to
renege.

Her name was Big Mama Chow. Big Mama was
fifty-eight years old, half Puerto Rican and half
Korean. She was Pitman's leading and only pros-
titute. Her liaisons with the Pitman undergraduates
helped her to supplement the income she received as
the vending machine refiller at the campus.

Her fee was always a flat rate. Thirty dollars per
half hour. This could mean three men at ten bucks
apiece, or six men at five apiece. Whatever went into
thirty equally. Big Mama didn't like to make change.

Back at Alpha Beta House, the five brothers had
finally scrounged up the necessary thirty dollars and
had decided, over two cases of Bud, that each would
take five minutes, giving Elmo a full ten minutes with
Big Mama. After all, it was *his* night.

Bob discovered early in his freshman year that beer
gave him hives the size of baseballs and, consequently, being the only sober brother, he was elected
to carry the money and do the driving.

Perhaps it was the construction out on Pitman Way, perhaps it was the speed at which they drove, whatever the reason, the ride was bumpy as hell. So bumpy, in fact, that, upon arriving at Big Mama's house, all the drinking brothers ran to the bushes to relieve themselves of the Cheetos and bean dip that had served as Elmo's "last supper."

Simultaneously, Big Mama opened the door to her modest wood-frame home and announced that the boys were on the clock and that the clock was ticking. "Who's first?" she said. Since Bob was the only Alpha Beta who wasn't busy "laughing at the lawn," he had no recourse but to answer, "I am."

Forty minutes later Bob came out Big Mama's front door, having given her the thirty bucks and his wristwatch as collateral for the other ten. He turned to face his now sobered and livid frat brothers. "I can explain," he explained.

"Fuck you," the brothers responded in unison.

Elmo went right past being pissed off into raging desperation. He pleaded with Big Mama for mercy. Big Mama pleaded poverty and slammed the door in Elmo's face. The evening was over.

The next day was one that Bob would remember for a long, long time. First, he was unanimously voted out of the Alpha Beta fraternity. Second, and much worse, while gathering his clothing and books off of the Alpha Beta front lawn, he was informed that Elmo's recruit bus had plunged into Pitman Ravine and that there were no survivors. Devastated beyond limits, he threw his belongings into the Camaro and headed for Dayton and Cathy.

Cathy knew something was wrong when the Camaro showed up unannounced, so she automatically slipped into the passenger seat in silence. They drove to the Dayton Reservoir to be alone. She hadn't seen Bob cry like this since the Joe Louis fiasco, and remembering that earlier incident, had a strong hunch as to what was called for. "Bob, is there anything I can do to make you feel better? I'll do anything," she whispered, and soon the sobbing was replaced by primal screams.

Bob never returned to Pitman, electing instead to remain close to Cathy until her graduation. His small off-campus apartment became their love nest, and all the previous rules and limitations on their sex life were replaced with the following:

1. Don't stop.
2. Marry me.

And that's exactly what Bob did. Three months after Cathy's graduation they exchanged their vows and headed off to Niagara Falls. Now all was legal and above board. And for Cathy, no more fun. Their wedding night at the Shangri-Lodge Motel was fraught with tension. Cathy just wasn't in the mood. Bob fought his frustration with his usual aplomb. He began crying hysterically and once again Cathy rose to the occasion with her now time-honored question. And so it went for several years. Bob found enough anxiety, tension, and turmoil in his life to allow for a good tear-induced slammer at least twice a week, and one night, after he totaled the car on the way home from a job from which he had just been fired, little Tracy was conceived.

This is but one example of White mating habits. The pathetic-husband approach works for Bob, but for others it may be one of the following:

1. A promise of new drapes.
2. Chilled Asti Spumante.
3. Sending the kids to camp.
4. Lying about wanting more children.
5. Lying about a terminal illness.
6. Hiring a new secretary.
7. Sticking poignant Ann Landers columns such as "Why Men Have Affairs" on the refrigerator with decorative magnets.

To many of you readers, Bob and Cathy's story may seem like pretty tame stuff. Perhaps it is because we sought to illustrate the ins and outs of White sex in a normal context, as performed by normal people. Our purpose is to educate the reader, not to get him off.

Of course, even among Whites, abnormalities will occur. There are a few grown White women out there who insert Ben-Wa balls before grocery shopping and dress up for an evening with their vibrators, and a few grown White men who keep two years' worth of *Penthouse* hidden in the garage inside the snow tires, hoping for a mild winter. We have even heard about a couple in Grand Rapids who spend their weekends dressing in scuba gear, eating out of dog dishes.

These people obviously do not regard sex as a means of reproduction. They are just having fun. And that kind of thinking is contrary to the whole concept of White sex.

74

# 6

## White Fright

We approach this chapter with some trepidation. Of course we do. What if we get it wrong? What if we get it right but people don't understand it? What if we can't finish it and they ask for our advance money back and we can't make our house payments and are forced to move into a small, dingy apartment where the gas stove isn't hooked up properly so the fumes cause brain damage in our kids so when they grow up they turn into criminals and embarrass us! It's enough to scare the bejesus out of you.

For most people on Earth, the fear of nuclear annihilation is the greatest fear of all. Not for White people. White people are in charge of nuclear annihilation. They'll push the buttons, they'll know it's coming, they'll be tucked away in their bomb shelters before it even makes the news.

Nor is The Unknown high on the list of White fears. Unlike the African native, the White man doesn't have to worry there's a mamba snake in the food supply. Unlike the igloo-dwelling Eskimo, he doesn't have to worry about an unseasonable hot spell. Unlike the Polish chef, he doesn't have to worry about how long to cook a three-minute egg.

For the White American, day-to-day survival is an unfearful given. The source of most of his doubts and worries is social. Where do I fit in? What do I talk about? What tie goes with what shirt? This can be a rough terrain in which to find your bearings, and thus White fears are often subtle, illusive, and as personal as fingerprints or dreams. In this case, of course, the dreams become nightmares.

To find out more about White nightmares, we took

76

our tape recorder out into the field. We asked select Whites to open up and tell us their worst nightmare, no matter how gruesome, bizarre, or embarrassing, as long as it fit on one side of a thirty-minute cassette.


## COMMAND PERFORMANCE

Our first taker: Bob Burk, ceiling tile salesman, Springfield, Indiana:

"I'm stopped on the street by our mayor, Hal Adams, who asks me to speak at the Rotary Club about my vacation to Cypress Gardens. Before I can answer him, a grapefruit-sized boil appears on the tip of my tongue. Hissoner smiles and tells me to have that removed and be at the dinner at seven thirty that night. The boil continues to grow to the size of a beach ball by midafternoon as I scurry around town looking for a doctor, to no avail. I try everything to remove it myself, from Blistex to a chain saw, but it only gets bigger. By dinnertime, it is the size of a weather balloon and I know I have to do something. I go with the obvious. I prepare a humorous speech about tongue boils, shower, and head off for the lodge, confident I will soon be basking in glory. No sooner do I reach the dais than I look down and see my balloon-size boil deflate with a swooshing sound and become a ham dinner, complete with baby peas and whipped potatoes. The next thing I know I am standing at the podium, reading my boil jokes, and look up to see an entire audience of boil-lipped Ro-

77

tarians scowling at me. I am mortified. Then the entire room turns into a ham dinner and my shoes start talking about Cypress Gardens and I wake up in a cold sweat."

## GREEK TRAGEDY

Sylvester Hinton, hairdresser, Cypress Gardens, Florida:
"I win a fabulous two-week, all-expense-paid trip to Greece on *Wheel of Fortune*. The moment I get there my member falls off."

## LIFE IN A VACUUM

Mrs. Frank Taylor, housewife, Hudson, Michigan:
"Frank calls from the office to say he's bringing his boss home for dinner. I panic. I set frozen chicken parts under warm running water and start to vacuum the living room. There's one spot on the carpeting that won't come out. I vacuum harder and harder, trying every attachment, but the spot stays there. I vacuum right through the carpeting and the living room floorboards and find myself in our basement, still after the same spot. It just won't go away! I refuse to give up and vacuum all the way through the center of the earth and find myself in China. Who should I run into but my husband, Frank, who's not working late at the office but having an affair with Nancy Kwan right before my very eyes. I attack her with the vacuum and manage to suck her completely

78

into the bag. Then comes the real nightmare. I realize the man is not my husband after all and the water is still running over the chicken parts. I run back through the center of the earth with my vacuum just in time to greet Frank and his boss at the door. They're starving. I hand Frank a box of Wheat Thins and dash into the kitchen, shaking uncontrollably. Then it hits me. I hit reverse on the vacuum, Nancy Kwan blows out in one piece, and together we fix a fabulous Chinese chicken salad. Then Frank and Nancy run through the hole in the living room floor and I never see them again."

## IF THE SHOE FITS

Kenny Kiner, shoe salesman, Bennet Falls, North Carolina:

"I'm fitting a middle-aged woman into a pair of sensible walking shoes when all of a sudden she pulls out a magic wand and taps me on the shoulder. I start shrinking until I'm only a half inch tall and find myself lodged between her big and first toes. Then I start shrinking even more 'til the hair on her toes looks like a stand of elms. I crawl out on her toenail and jump to the floor and land in some gum. I'm starving by now, so I break off a piece of the gum and start chewing it like crazy. I blow a bubble big enough to climb into and float out the shoe store window all the way into outer space, where I get stuck on the side of a sports network satellite. I can't stand sports announcers so I blow on my tiny little thumb until I'm dead."

## ACCORDION TO THE RULES

Bridgette Ridgely, beauty contest contestant, Claremont, California:

"It's the talent segment of the semifinal regionals for Miss California and I can't find my accordion. I'm still in my bathing suit from the previous segment, but I don't care. I have to find my accordion. Then all of a sudden I'm in this huge room full of accordions, but none of them is mine and they're all laughing at me like in a Walt Disney movie. I realize as I turn around that the judges have been watching the whole thing, so I tell them that my talent is experimental theater. They all just stare at me and give the prize to a Vietnamese girl who's only four feet tall, and when I bend over to give her a congratulatory hug I break wind, which in real life I never do."

The nightmare is, of course, the most grandiose form of fear, and, as you have just read, it can be downright bone-chilling. However, lesser fears and phobias also run rampant through the White community. These span the spectrum from the often fantasy-oriented "What if's" to the pragmatic and tooth-grinding "Oh no, I'm going to have to's."

Let us examine some "What if's" to start with. We selected one hundred White people at random and came up with these as the most popular responses. Sort of like they do on *Family Feud*.

1. What if the neighbors find out we have a pool table?

2. What if our daughter marries a non-White and he's not the nice kind of non-White like we hired two of down at our office?
3. What if nobody comes to our garage sale and we have to cart all of this shit back down into the basement?
4. What if they already have one?
5. What if your parents remember the "overdue book incident" when you were fourteen, and all of a sudden you are *not* in the will?
6. What if they really weren't with the Negro College Fund and we never see the magazines?
7. What if they don't take Visa?
8. What if her mother needs CPR?
9. What if it isn't "just a rash"?

So much for the "What if's." Needless to say there are thousands of them, and White folks deal with them on a daily basis. Let's take a gander at some of the more complex "Oh no, I'm going to have to's."

1. Oh no, I'm going to have to pump my own gas!
2. Oh no, I'm going to have to eat it without mayonnaise!
3. Oh no, I'm going to have to dance!
4. Oh no, I'm going to have to order in French!
5. Oh no, I'm going to have to say grace!
6. Oh no, I'm going to have to remember the Pledge of Allegiance!
7. Oh no, I'm going to have to change maids!
8. Oh no, I'm going to have to use chopsticks!

9. Oh no, I'm going to have to vote!
10. Oh no, I'm going to have to carve the turkey!

To some, the foregoing fears are simple to overcome; for others, they are the source of award-winning anxiety attacks that can send you straight to the hospital emergency ward, which is, in itself, a source of great anxiety for most White people. Spending two and a half hours on a sticky green vinyl seat next to an illegal alien with a garden rake imbedded in his skull just so you can describe your symptoms to a Pakistani intern is hardly referred to in White circles as a "night out." Still, sticking it out has its rewards. You could walk away with a substantial supply of Valium. Valium, incidentally, does not inhibit Whiteness; on the contrary, it increases it. The mere fact that you cannot operate heavy machinery is proof enough.

# 7
## White Lies

Despite the fact that all of our presidents have been White, lying is not the sole province of White people. To say that it is would be lying. The truth is that everyone, at some time or another, tells lies.

It is generally agreed that lying is at most a cardinal sin and at least naughty, yet it persists. It not only has existed as long as the history of mankind, but has altered the course of history as well.

If it wasn't for lying, Julius and Ethel Rosenberg would be running a kosher catering service in the Bronx; we would be celebrating Judas' birthday on December 25; and Joan Collins would be riding the bus for half fare.

There are big lies like "it's a clean bomb," "we're putting you in here for your own good," and "when you die, you will go to heaven," but there are also hundreds of little lies. We call these White lies. A White lie is any bending, contorting, or avoiding of the truth that can't be explained by adding "Hey, I was just kidding!"

For White people, White lying can hold the key to job security as well as help maintain a solid marriage and bolster the confidence of less than extraordinary children. It can explain tardiness at functions, earliness at functions, and absence at functions. It can turn neighbors into "friends." It can preserve great institutions like the two-party system, seeing your dentist twice a year, and Mother's Day.

A good White lie can also save your ass, and, after a couple of beers, it won't eat at you for saying it. More important, it may be the only time in the average White person's life that he uses his imagination.

Often the White lie can serve as an icebreaker when White people find themselves forced into conversation with each other. Lying right off the bat establishes a certain trust, a trust based on the tacitly understood premise that neither party will resort to the truth, therefore no one will get hurt. An example of this might be:

*White Woman 1:* "Helen, I've never seen you looking better!"
*White Woman 2:* "Me? You should talk! You haven't aged a day since high school!!"

Another example:

*White Man 1:* "Jesus, Frank, how much have you lost? Twenty pounds?!!"
*White Man 2:* "Twenty-five!"

One need only open his ears and he will be astounded by the amount of insincerity with which we are bombarded on any given day. The following remarks were heard in the course of one afternoon alone:

1. "Just let me know if that's too much air on you folks in the backseat."
2. "No problem at all, sometimes I *like* to drink it black."
3. "I can't believe you built this yourself!"
4. "You'd never know that was a wig."
5. "We were watching PBS."

6. "We waited until we were married."
7. "I *love* Christmas!"
8. "It looks like you bought it in a store."
9. "It's been fourteen years and it's still like a honeymoon."
10. "I love what you've done with the kitchen."
11. "I have no real feelings about it, one way or the other."
12. "We have a lot of Black friends."
13. "I can always ask my brother for the money."
14. "One more cup won't keep me awake."
15. "I've got to hang up now, there's someone at the door."

Despite the innocuousness and timidity of lies like the ones listed above, a White lie can still be a dangerous thing when misplaced, ill conceived, or spoken in thoughtless haste. We are all well familiar with the story of the boy who cried "wolf." He got eaten or scratched up or something like that, it's a little blurry right now, but he didn't come out very well. The following story is not as well known but may point out the dangers of the White lie even better for our White readers.

## *TOM'S BIG MISTAKE*

Tom Connery started in the mail room at Motivation "R" Us fourteen years ago. Since then, thanks to diligence and an eye for the almighty dollar, he has risen to the rank of junior vice president. This position obviously demands extra work and an occasional late night at the office. Tracy Connery was accustomed to this. She knew that making special dinners at ten thirty P.M. for a weary Tom was all part of providing her daughter with a new Rabbit convertible on her sixteenth birthday.

It was not unusual for Tom to call at night and announce that "he'd be a little late." Tom, however, was not slaving late over an expense account or inventory report. As it turns out, his new secretary, Gidget, had announced over lunch that she was studying Swedish massage. Tom immediately confessed to a lot of tension in his shoulder muscles and plans were laid to take an extra hour after work to alleviate the problem. Since Tom's office was not equipped with a massage table, it would be necessary to go to Gidget's apartment for the rub. Even though it was a scant three blocks from the office, Tom felt the need for another call home. "Hi, it's me. Listen, they just threw another stack of invoices at me. It could be ten, maybe eleven tonight. Okay, me too, honey."

After sharing two bottles of Almadén rosé, Tom finally felt comfortable enough to strip down to his Expand-A-Belt shorts and assume the position on the massage table. Gidget brought out an assortment of scented vegetable oils and the massage began. The rub was soft and soothing at first, and then got progressively deeper as Gidget moved toward the problematic shoulder area. It was problematic for two reasons: first, it actually *was* tighter than a ketchup cap, and, second, Tom's shoulders were so hairy that any deep rubbing pulled the hairs in such a way that the result was more like torture than relief. It was nearly eight o'clock before this latter problem was realized.

Meanwhile, at the Connery household, Tracy had her own problems. Tom's mother, who had been their "house guest" for the past nine months, got a Scrabble tile lodged in her throat. Through garbled rasping she explained, "It was right next to the Wheat Thins and I guess I didn't really look."

After futile attempts to retrieve the little tile with tweezers, crochet needles, and a loop of Scotch tape, it was decided that a trip to the local emergency ward was called for. The problem now became what to do about a baby-sitter for the children while Tracy was gone.

Like any responsible White person, Tracy immediately turned to the Yellow Pages for help. An advertisement for a group called Baby, It's You, Inc. immediately caught her eye, and, rather than look any farther, she dialed the number and was assured that someone would be there in moments. Tracy thought it a little strange that they accepted Master-Charge but was so relieved to have someone on such short notice that she didn't stop to question it.

Twelve minutes later the doorbell rang and Tracy was stunned by what she saw. Her "sitter" was a six-foot-three-inch well-muscled Adonis in a tank top, tight leather pants, with a bathrobe under his arm. She was doubly stunned when he said "Hello" and began running his fingers through her hair. Tracy quickly ushered the would-be sexual surrogate into the foyer, well out of the view and earshot of her gagging mother-in-law and curious children.

She explained to him, as quickly and exactly as possible, the nature of her problem and her obvious misunderstanding of the "services" offered by Baby, It's You, Inc. Her "gentleman caller" understood completely. He was in fact relieved. "I'd much rather watch the children," he said. At this point, Tracy's concern for the well-being of her fourteen-year-old daughter was alleviated by his speech pattern. He was obviously as gay as a sunset. As for her son, she simply prayed that the T'ai Chi lessons on a year's worth of Sunday mornings would pay off in a crisis.

She wrapped Grandma in a down comforter, grabbed her car keys, and told the children, "I'm taking Grandma out for some air, you guys just keep on playing your game." Another little White lie. Her children bought it, however, only adding, "Hey! Where's the 'X'?"

Tom had removed his watch at the request of his secretary/masseuse and had no idea that it was nearly ten o'clock when the drunken decision was made to shave his back. To make it more tolerable and relaxing, Gidget put on some Johnny Mathis music and then started scraping with her Lady Schick. Tom lay on the table as limp as a slug, intoxicated by the Almadén, the smell of the pine-scented lather, and found himself actually harmonizing with Johnny on "Chances Are."

Ironically enough, a Muzak version of "Chances

Are" was being piped into the emergency ward of Hawkins Falls Sinai Hospital at the very moment that Tracy and her rasping mother-in-law arrived. After Tracy had made it through two issues of *People*, a doctor emerged from within and escorted Mrs. Connery to surgery. Dr. Ngo Kdn (pronounced, honest to God, "no kiddin'"), a young Laotian intern, was able to retrieve the elusive Scrabble tile with chopsticks that had been provided with his take-out dinner. His inscrutable eye, however, also noted some severe laceration of the uvula, and he was concerned. In his broken English he described it to Mrs. Connery as looking like "a hamburger raindrop sitting on your tongue." The decision was made to keep Mrs. Connery overnight for further observation. Tracy signed the appropriate release forms and dashed home.

Gidget had never shaved a man's back before. She had never shaved a man's anything before, so she was unaccustomed to such things as aerosol shave cream and its proper usage. Tom's back looked like a huge pile of foamy cauliflower. She could barely push the razor through the suds. The decision was made to rinse him down with soothing warm water. The result was a thoroughly clean back and extremely drenched Expand-A-Belt shorts. Tom, by now reasonably snockered by the Almadén, tore off the shorts in a cavalier manner and grabbed a dish towel to cover his manhood.

Tracy arrived home moments later to find her children happily completing the Scrabble game with the gentleman they had come to know as "Libra." All seemed well. She called her husband at the office; there was no answer, so she figured he'd be home any minute. The office was only eight blocks away and the children seemed content, so what could be lost by driving Libra home and saving the expense of his car fare? "Daddy will be here in a sec," she told the children as she and the young hunk headed out the front door.

Gidget soon realized that shaving someone's back quickly obviates the need for protocol and ceremony. She was also drenched from the rinsing water and, with the social freedom back-shaving afforded her, she decided to doff her drenched duds as well. Right down to her undies. Tom got a fleeting glimpse of the word "Friday" embroidered on her bikini briefs and immediately felt a great loss of tension in his shoulders. "Maybe there *is* something to this massage," he thought.

Tracy and Libra talked freely on the way to his apartment, he more than she. He gave her his recipe for quiche, told her about a rendezvous he had had with a stuntman who was too afraid to admit his leanings, and, ultimately, confessed that he didn't have change for the twenty-dollar bill that Tracy offered him for his twelve-dollar service.

"I've got change upstairs," he said, "and I'd love to show you the drapes I made for the bathroom." Since parking was easy, and the neighborhood well lit, Tracy felt no problem in going up to Libra's apartment. It was two minutes out of her life and she could save eight dollars, the price of a ham. Libra confessed that he had a roommate. A woman roommate. "It's easier that way," he said, and added, "But we should be kinda quiet, she's usually asleep by ten."

She wasn't asleep. She was in the midst of a great, seminude, aerosol shaving cream fight with her boss, Tom Connery. Tom got her a good one right on the stomach and she whirled and got him back. Tom slipped on the foamy floorboards and fell to his knees. Gidget seized the moment and jumped aboard, "horsey" style, and started squirting the back of his head with shaving cream. Their squeals of laughter were interrupted by the sound of the opening door and the sight of Libra and Tracy. Tom immediately shot himself in the face with the shaving cream as an attempt at disguise, but Tracy knew it was him the minute his towel fell.

It took the better part of six months for Tom and Tracy Connery to iron out this little misunderstanding. Every problem has a solution, however, if it can be faced by two reasonable adults who are willing to listen to what the other has to say. The Connery crisis was no different. Tracy got the house and custody of the children. Tom got the lawn mower and most of his own clothes. Both got a rude awakening as to the power of "little White lies."

A brief postscript: Gidget took her two weeks' severance pay and enrolled in a local cosmetology college. Libra settled down with his stuntman friend and they began a successful Lhasa Apso grooming service.

The elder Mrs. Connery's uvula couldn't be saved and was surgically removed by Dr. Ngo Kdn. She now communicates by spelling out her thoughts with Scrabble tiles that she carries in a bag by her side.

# 8
## White Food

Food plays a big part in the White person's diet. Unlike the French, the Italians, and the Mexicans, who treat every meal like a work of culinary art, the White American reserves his food artistry for special occasions, sometimes up to three a year. For his day-to-day regimen, he's looking for something simple to fix, easy to eat, and bulky enough to fill him up.

Why should the White man bother with a fancy breakfast when a couple of Pop-Tarts can hold you over just fine until you get to the donuts at the office? Why go out for an elaborate lunch when you can bring in two Big Macs and a pound of fries and munch on them while you dictate that inventory report? And dinner—some people spend hours languishing over the evening meal and miss every one of the good shows. What a waste! White people simply snack on beer and beer nuts with Dan Rather until Gino arrives with a couple of large cheese-only pizzas. Out come the TV trays, grab some more beer and napkins from the kitchen, and dinner is served without ever missing a beat of *Match Game PM* or *Dynasty*.

But what about those fancy White meals we mentioned earlier? When White people do it up right, it is a gastronomic breathtaker. And well it should be. It is the culmination of generations of hand-me-down menu tips, volumes of clippings from *Good Housekeeping, Family Circle*, and the Thursday edition of the local newspaper, hundreds of three-by-five-inch file card recipes, and a never-ending stream of new and advanced labor-saving kitchen appliances. Put this collected body of knowledge in the hands of a capable housewife, her two daughters, and her visiting mother, and you will see a spread that puts the Last Supper to shame.

If you have never had the good fortune to visit a White family's home on a holiday like Thanksgiving, you don't know what you've missed. Here's what you've missed:

## APPETIZERS

The appetizer is the first lap in the holiday eat-a-thon. Here's why. The main dish, usually a turkey or a ham, takes four or five hours to cook thoroughly, which means if you get it in by ten, you won't be eating until three or four in the afternoon. The Detroit-Dallas game usually starts at one and when the men gather around the set, they need something to put in their bellies besides beer. Still, you don't want to fill them up and ruin their dinner. Enter the appetizer.

Cream Cheese–Filled Celery "Boats"
(with paprika for color)

Ruffles and Dip
(a quart of sour cream, a package of
Lipton's onion soup mix, and a half cup
of sugar, blend with a spatula)

Hickory Farms Cheese Balls

Bite-Size Individual Pizzas

Velveeta Squares on Toothpicks,
with Assorted Crackers:

Triscuits
Wheat Thins
Ritz
Waverly Wafers
Sociables
Saltines

Cocktail Wieners
(with French's mild mustard)

Pretzel Sticks

Potato Sticks

Bridge Mix, aka Party Mix
(Rice Chex, Wheat Chex, Corn Chex,
peanuts, corn nuts, walnuts, olives)

Melon Balls

Gumdrop Tree
(for the young and young-at-heart)

Just enough to whet the appetite for the first course.

## FIRST COURSE

The first course serves many purposes. It's something to eat right after grace. It kills time while the host is grappling with carving the turkey and taking orders for white and dark. It is usually pretty to look at, so the hostess gets some important compliments right up front. And, last, it allows time for the potatoes to finish boiling.

Ambrosia
(miniature marshmallows, Jell-O custard, mayonnaise, Del Monte fruit cocktail, topped with shredded coconut)

Large Molded Jell-O Bunny
(with raisin eyes, in a "hutch" of iceberg lettuce leaves)

Cold Beet Platter

Deviled Eggs
(with paprika for color)

Cherry Tomato "Roses"
(time-consuming but worth it)

99

And now for the body of the meal.

## THE MAIN COURSE

### Les Legumes*

Boiled Birds Eye Green Beans

Boiled Birds Eye Cauliflower

Boiled Birds Eye Asparagus

Boiled Birds Eye Carrots

Boiled Del Monte Turnips

Boiled Potatoes

(all of the above with cheese sauce)

### The Turkey

The turkey is what everyone came for. That's why they call it "Turkey Day." It has to be done to a turn, and most important, it has to be *done*. Ask any White person and he'll tell you that "you can't cook a turkey too long, if it's a little dry that's what the gravy's for."

More importantly to some, old Tom is just wrapping for the stuffing. Everyone loves stuffing, and the people at Stove Top know it. Before the advent of Stove Top stuffing, which is always moist, people had to drench their stuffing with gravy, often leaving little

*The vegetables.

**100**

or no gravy to keep the turkey from tasting like a Buxton wallet.

Little white paper "panties" on the turkey's feet give a festive touch. These are not to be eaten.

### The Fixin's

Stove Top Stuffing

Ocean Spray Canned Cranberry Sauce
(sliced, with parsley garni)

Gravy
(one tureen per diner)

Candied Yams and Honey

Minute Rice
(or Rice-A-Roni where available)

Brown-and-Serve Rolls
with Assorted Jams, Jellies, and Preserves
Individual Butter Pats

Now comes naptime, but the meal is not over. As soon as everyone is back on their feet and well over that woozy feeling, they'll be clamoring for the finale. The desserts.

### THE DESSERTS

Pumpkin Pie with Cool Whip

Mincemeat Pie with Cool Whip

Rhubarb Pie with Cool Whip

Pecan Pie with Cool Whip

Chocolate Brownies with Cool Whip

Lemon Sponge Cake with Cool Whip

Butter Brickle Ice Cream Sundaes
(ice cream, peanuts, Maraschino cherry,
and Cool Whip)

Maxwell House Decaf and Hard Candy

What a feast! And certainly enough for everyone. And wouldn't it be nice to think that everyone shares in it equally. Such is not the case. Remember, these are White people.

Uncle Walter has a duodenal ulcer, which he still blames on the Eisenhower Administration. Consequently, he spent the entire meal beating his potatoes and vegetables into a digestible paste, and missed out on the turkey altogether.

Aunt Fay decided three years ago that all living things, both plant and animal, were sacred, and thus refused to eat anything but the brown-and-serve rolls, the Stove Top stuffing, the Velveeta cheese squares, and the Cool Whip.

Darlene, seventeen, with an eye toward a modeling career, had two melon balls and most of the cold beet platter before excusing herself to the bathroom.

Little Kendall, age twelve, enlightened the whole table as to how turkeys are actually killed and dressed, causing a bank run on the Jell-O mold and the boiled vegetables.

102

Cousin Larry, an inveterate pipe smoker, had an unfortunate coughing spasm that resulted in a major goober landing atop of the turnips. He felt obliged to eat the entire bowl himself, leaving no room for turkey.

Grandmother, who at eighty-six still insists on doing everything herself, spilled a pitcher of Tang all over the turkey and stuffing, and by the time this space-age beverage was sufficiently toweled off, everyone was onto dessert.

The untouched turkey at this meal was not wasted. It was ultimately consumed by the hostess and family over the next four weeks in the form of sandwiches, croquettes, casseroles, soups, and dog food. Then it was time for the big Christmas turkey, with all the fixin's.

"Good food, good meat, good God, let's eat."*

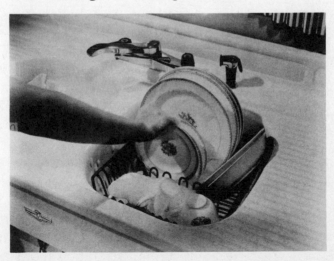

*Traditional White grace.

# 9
## Whites at Leisure

Unless your last name is Rockefeller, Guggenheim, or DeLorean, you probably work for a living. So do most White people. Some Whites, of course, are descended from the original patent holders on such items as the nonskid rubber crutch tip or fruit-flavored envelope glue and have never worked a day in their lives. They are the lucky ones. For the rest of White America it's forty hours a week at the old grind. Grueling as it may be, it still leaves 128 hours a week for "leisure activities."

Leisure time, or "quality time," as it is currently referred to, is quintessential to the White way of life. It can be as simple and relaxing as cracking open a new Jacqueline Susann novel in the backyard hammock, or as energy-consuming as a rousing game of horseshoes. It can be as inexpensive as napping or as costly as cat breeding. It can be as quiet as embroidery or as cacophonous as remodeling the basement. But it must exist somewhere during every White week or weekend. Without it the White spirit would shrivel up and die, like a smelt on a hot beach.

Let's examine some leisure activities peculiar to White culture.

### GOLF

Golf is the consuming passion of millions of White Americans, and why shouldn't it be? The list of reasons for its abiding popularity is endless, but we'll keep it at ten.

1. It's played outdoors, so your face and hands can get tan.
2. It affords the opportunity to dress up in colors you'd never dream of wearing to the office.
3. The ball isn't heavy and you can hire someone to carry the clubs.
4. You can drink and smoke, continuously.
5. You can be on the links by 6 A.M., three hours before your wife wakes up with a mile-long list of things to do around the house.
6. You're allowed to hit something with all your might and pretend it's someone who's been driving you nuts.
7. You don't have to be in shape.
8. You can practice putting in your office.
9. You can cheat.
10. You can make a shitload of money if you're really good at it.

Let's take a closer look at reason number 2, the one about clothes, since it not only applies to golf but to many other White leisure activities. It may seem like small potatoes to some, but to many Whites, the right kind of sports clothing, or "togs," is the ticket to boldness and adventure in life.

During the work week, most White male apparel is limited to a meager color spectrum. Generally, it's light tan to dark gray. Nothing else is really acceptable in the "get along to get ahead" world of work. A navy suit for awards banquets and funerals might complete the wardrobe, but that's about it.

The lady of the house keeps it pretty simple, too, as

she goes about her daily life. Loose-fitting slacks and a Ship'N Shore blouse for every day. (Some prefer the all-purpose mumu.) Rubber gloves for gardening and dishwashing, and a simple, modest cream or "off-cream" polyester dress for afternoon get-togethers. Since Mom spends a lot of time on her feet, "sensible shoes" are the order of the day, supplemented by fuzzy house slippers, the order of the night and morning.

Then comes the weekend and it's like opening a box of Crayolas.

Mom is off to tennis in a bright yellow ensemble straight out of the Ice Follies. Her normally modest skirt length is replaced by a "Chrissy Evert" micro-skirt that shows off her tricot-lined lace panties at every backhand. Who cares if the backs of her thighs resemble a relief map of the world's great rivers? She's in heaven. She feels like Lady Godiva with a Prince racket, and she's maybe even lost a pound or two. She'll find out. She'll weigh herself immediately following the match.

Dad, on the other hand, can't wait to show off his sports duds to the guys out at the country club. Emulating his favorite sports figures, he's wearing his Arnold Palmer chartreuse alpaca golf sweater, his Bear Bryant orange porkpie hat, and the red-and-white checker pants, erroneously called "jackass pants" by detractors, that he saw Gerald Ford wearing last spring at the Crosby. All of this, of course, is offset with just the right touch of White. A White belt. White shoes. And a White golf glove, casually hanging out of his back pocket.

The fun doesn't stop there. Dad always rents the shiniest blue tux with the powder-blue frill shirt for the annual club dinner-dance, and has an ample supply of madras Bermudas and printed Dacron shirts for any summer outing. Mom collects party aprons that literally spell out a good time—"Hot Stuff—Not the Food, Silly, ME!!!" or "Are We Having Fun Yet?"—and loves to don her favorite rhinestone sunglasses with the saucy Day-Glo pink holders to add pizzazz to a Sunday drive.

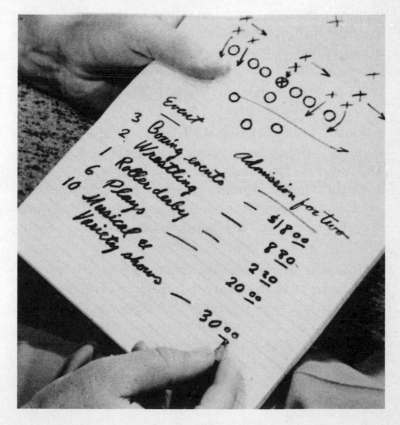

Leisure is full-time work among Whites. Day in and day out, there's always something to do. To illustrate this, we followed the Hal Harrison family (see Chapter Three) through a typical week of leisure-time activities. Here's how it broke down:

MONDAY. Joyce, Hal's wife, spent the day making brownies for Debby's after-school Pep Club meeting and sewing Tommy's Abe Lincoln outfit for the school play, "That Man from Springfield." Of course, she has her own hobby, refinishing floors. Hal played racquetball at lunch and later threw his back out showing Tommy how to do a reverse lay-up in the driveway. They all got together after dinner for a rousing three-hour game of Go Fish.

TUESDAY. This is Debby's big day—local gymnastics tryouts, balance beam competition, floor level. Hal and Joyce were proud of her twelfth-place finish, but a tearful Debby announced she was switching to a modeling career. Tommy couldn't attend; he was busy lowering the backboard so he could slam-dunk.

WEDNESDAY. Joyce took the morning off for her bowling league and floral arranging class. Hal took the afternoon off to play eighteen holes of golf. Tommy dropped out of the school play and played Donkey Kong in the 7-11 for four hours. Debby had a piano lesson before school, student government at lunch, Future Homemakers after school, and Tri-Hi-Y in the evening. She changed her clothes seven times.

THURSDAY. Thursday is Joyce's Homemakers Club Day, and it was her turn this week, so no one could touch any of the cold cuts in the icebox or come home until after five. Hal dropped by Arnie's Sports Shop and bought a new water-hazard ball fetcher and a year's supply of fishing hooks. Debby went shopping for clothes. Tommy got home about eleven. (After baseball practice, he decided to do his homework at the miniature golf course, where they also have Donkey Kong.)

FRIDAY. The last day before the weekend. Joyce stocked up on Cheetos, Cheez-Its, Cheese Whiz, and Tab, Hal gassed up the car and cleaned the Weber barbecue, Tommy got out the cable guide to circle the dirty movies, and Debby bought more clothes. Hal enjoyed joking with Debby's friends at her slumber party, giving Joyce some free time to read *People* and watch Barbara Walters's fascinating interview with Betty Ford.

SATURDAY. 6 A.M. Hal to golf course. 8 A.M. Debby on all-day swimming trip to Lake Watonka. 10 A.M. Mom takes Tommy to Little League game. 12 A.M. Mom takes Tommy to McDonald's. 1 P.M. Mom takes Tommy to movies. 2 P.M. Hal returns from golf, starts the grill. 3 P.M. Mom back from Aerobics, Debby back from lake, Tommy back from movies, friends arrive, barbecue begins. 5 P.M. Badminton. 6 P.M. Homemade ice cream attempted. 6:30 P.M. Hal sent to store for real ice cream. 7 P.M. Charades. 9 P.M. Party's over, Debby heads for *Porky's III* with current Romeo; Hal and

111

Joyce, slightly tipsy, sneak off to their room; Tommy tunes in cable TV.

SUNDAY. After church, the family drives to Aunt Millie and Uncle Pete's for Sunday dinner and a nice "visit." One ham and two NFL games later, they head home, just in time for *60 Minutes*. Hal falls asleep in his La-Z-Boy. Debby chooses her wardrobe for Monday and Joyce refinishes the floor in the den.

Whew! That's some fun-filled week, enough to exhaust an average family, but not the Harrisons. First of all, they try to stay healthy, which isn't easy with all that fun food around. They try to pace themselves to avoid the kind of scheduling conflicts that make tempers flare. Notice, for instance, how Hal's golf game doesn't interfere with Joyce's chauffeuring Tommy on Saturday. And, finally, they don't let things like depressing world events or time-consuming do-good projects or worries about the future disturb their commitment to a happy and eventful recreational life.

Now there's a lesson we can all profit from.

# 10

# The Happy Face

White people love symbols for things. In that a symbol is a smaller, distilled, nonverbal advertisement of a larger, much more complex and abstract idea, it is of little wonder that they are so embraced by Whites. Just as the male peacock spreads his fantail and is instantly recognized as seriously amorous, so too can the White man express himself through symbols.

It's so simple. A small enameled flag on one's lapel declares patriotism, and a circle pin on a teenage girl's sweater proclaims she's still Daddy's little girl. A tiny cloisonné tie tack can successfully tell the world about one's dedication to the Kiwanis International, the Lions Club, or the BPOE. A small appliqué on his uniform lets everyone know that at least one eleven-year-old Cub Scout knows his knots. A Spiedel Ident-o-Band bracelet can remind even the most dim-witted owner of his own name.

These merry clip-ons, add-ons, pin-ons, iron-ons, sew-ons, and so on provide instant communication in our contemporary society. However, the need for symbols goes way back. Hundreds, if not thousands of years ago, men devised clever symbols to declare their presence on Earth and perhaps their happiness. Of course, their symbols weren't as complex, artful, or specific as, say, today's Sam the Eagle Olympic booster pin, but they did the best they could with what they had.

And what did they have? Well, the Egyptians, for example, had enough limestone to give half the grown male population double hernias and used it to make a sphinx that no one understands to this day.

And those Aborigines that used to live on Easter Island obviously spent their summer vacation erecting long, stone sculptures of John Carradine's face; unless you're Keith or David, it probably doesn't mean much. Once again, what good is a symbol if you don't know what it symbolizes?

Leonardo da Vinci, whom every Italian-American claims is a genius, if not a relative, may have had his finger on it when he painted the Mona Lisa, a simple smiling face. But for all his genius, he missed the boat. The smile wasn't big enough. It has to be restored all the time, and it's hard to fit on your lapel.

If Leonardo had only broadened Mona's enigmatic grin, simplified the background, and painted the whole face yellow, he'd still be in the chips today. He'd own the copyright on this little sucker.

The happy face. You recognized him right away. Why? Because he's your friend. And how did he become your friend? Like anyone else would. By seeing him constantly, on a day-in, day-out basis, in the most pleasant of situations.

He's there on your coffee cup in the morning, and perhaps on the milk carton as well. He's on your daughter's lunch bucket as she heads off for school. He's on the bumper of your wife's car that you had to take that day. He's on the dry cleaner's window when you pick up your shirts and on the plastic bag they

**115**

come in. He's on the back of buses, trucks, and ambulances. He's on your boss's door, along with "Thanks for Not Smoking." And he's on your cocktail napkins before you head home to find him on your sheets and drapes. He's there for one reason and one reason only. To tell you to have a nice day. Something a lot of us forget to tell each other.

If you're like millions of White people, you adore him and wish he could be everywhere. Not just in the United States, where most of us have a nice day anyway, but all over the world, including those places where cocker spaniels are an entrée and flies crawl on your face and it doesn't seem to bother you.

It's a hell of an idea—the happy face around the world. It could spread joy, it could spread happiness, and for the White entrepreneur who picks up the ball and runs with it, it could spell "mansion in Santa Barbara with a Rolls in the drive."

Our staff set about the task of adapting the happy face to other cultures. The following, fully copyrighted (worldwide) images are the result of their diligent efforts.

*ENGLAND*

To the White American, England comes about as close as anywhere to being an acceptable country.

When the White American takes a trip to Europe, or perhaps wins one on *Jeopardy*, it is usually to England. This is not to say that an English White person is to be confused with an American White person. Let's face it, there is only one beverage to sip while perusing the morning sports pages and it sure as hell ain't tea.

Calling a spade a spade, the White American traveler to England is faced with a meaningless queen, an even more bumbling parliament, yellow teeth, and a nation full of working-class people who insist on referring to a sixteen-wheel tractor trailer as a "lorry." Still we wish them happiness.

## CANADA

Canada is basically Yugoslavia without all the flash and glamour. Take away their Canada Dry Ginger Ale, Canadian Club, and Canadian bacon and you've got a bunch of hockey players living in igloos. The only time they ever even get into the pages of *People* magazine is when Margaret Trudeau bends over at Studio 54, which is in America. Still it's a more than defendable border, and we wish them the best.

## AUSTRALIA

Twenty some-odd years ago my high school geography teacher told me that Australia had its winter during our summer. That was twenty years ago and they still haven't gotten it right. They send us Olivia Newton-John and Helen Reddy and think they're doing us a favor! The happy face might just smart up our friends down under. G'day!

## INDIA

Boy, could India use a happy face. They could benefit greatly from "having a nice day." They also could "use a break today" except that there are no McDonald's because they won't eat beef. They treat cows like White people treat parakeets. Ask any self-respecting White woman how she feels about having a bale of hay and a salt lick in her living room and you'll get a pretty good idea why there are no White people in India. Perhaps a happy symbol might help.

## GERMANY*

White people don't visit Germany unless they are drafted into the service or think they can get a deal on a Mercedes.

## AFRICA

The first problem with this idea is, what would your average Watusi pin it on? The second problem is teaching them not to worship it. The answer to problem number 1: Replace the traditional pin with Velcro. They could stick it to their hair for special occasions. The answer to problem number 2 is what we've been screaming at them for decades: education, education, education. Of course, if you're Caucasian and live in South Africa, you should refer to Germany.

*This is also the official happy face of Argentina.

## *ISRAEL*

This happy little mensch might be just the ticket for peace in the Middle East. As the Jewish people themselves say, "It can't hoit!!" Too bad Mr. Happy Face doesn't have a nose, we could have had a real field day!!

## *ITALY*

Here's a postcard we received from some White people who were visiting Italy.

Dear friends,

Well, here we are in Rome, Italy. We've spent the last two days just sitting here in our Holiday Inn waiting for our flight back home. We got one of those Super-Savers and we can't leave until Friday. At least our hotel is clean and new. The rest of this town looks like it's falling down. It's in ruins!! Also, is it too much

to expect that people speak English when we're
spending this kind of money? We don't think
so! Speaking of money, you should see theirs.
It's hilarious. Room service is at the door with
our BLTs, so got to go for now. Chow!
XXXOOOO to all of you.

The Butler family

## CHINA

This one's a natural. He's already yellow. More important, I think we all agree that we would like the
Chinese to be happy. We certainly don't want to see
them mad. There's billions of them, and once they
started that spinning and kicking stuff that they do in
their movies, we'd be no match. Too bad Nixon didn't
have pockets full of these little buttons to pass out to
the children when he visited. White tourists could
even leave them as tips, since the Chinese are all
Communists and don't have any money anyway.

## JAPAN

If you are young, White, and aggressive, you might envision making a small bundle selling these trinkets in Tokyo. Forget it. You might sell *one*. Fifteen minutes later the buyer will have figured out a way to make it cheaper, change something about it so he can own the copyright, and give thousands of people a job for life making them. Worse yet, you turn the button over and see that it's been made out of an old Star Kist tuna fish can. But that's what makes them Japanese. They can go through a White person's garbage and build a radio.

## THE HAPPY FACE CONTEST

By now I'm sure the wheels in your head are turning. You're saying, "What about Panama, Sri Lanka, the Falkland Islands? They could use a happy face, too!"

Right you are, and you may be just the person to

think it up. We've supplied the circle, you supply the innards. Just follow these simple rules. After that it's up to you.

1. No Communist countries.
2. No erasing.

Winners will be judged on the basis of neatness, originality of thought, and attention span.

Here's your chance to be the proud owner of a closet full of Expand-A-Belt fashions. All entries must be postmarked no later than December 31, 1959. Good luck!

# 11
## White Death

This is not the title of a new shark movie. It is a very serious subject.

For most White people, who seem to embrace the "I'm going to live forever" philosophy, dying is something that grandparents do. Reaching a ripe old age before "buying the ranch" is a commonly shared White goal. To this end, White people spend their lives driving slowly in a passing lane, avoiding certain parts of town after dark, taking Geritol and One-A-Day vitamins, seeing their dentist twice a year, and seeking desk jobs when conscripted into the military.

Every minority group treats death in its own peculiar manner. The Indians dunk their dead in lighter fluid and send them smoking down the Ganges, in hopes they'll return as cows and make the world a better place. The Irish have "wakes," where everyone gets so drunk that, by evening's end, you can't tell the corpse from the mourners. In parts of New Guinea the deceased is deboned and served on a bed of leaf lettuce. The White person is no less unique and inventive. It is *he* who created the concept and practice of the eulogy.

Before we proceed further and actually hear a White eulogy, it is important to note that, especially during times of grief, the words "dead" and "died" are anathema to Whites. The preferred terms are any of the following:

1. Gone to meet his maker.
2. In a better place.
3. Expired.
4. Deceased.

5. No longer with us.
6. Finally at peace.
7. Late.
8. Passed away.
9. Up in heaven.
10. Moved to Vermont. (Used when explaining death to a small child.)

Likewise, the following terms should *not* be used in the presence of the immediate family for at least three weeks:

1. Ate the big one.
2. Bought it.
3. Went south on us.
4. Bellied up.
5. Checked out.
6. Keeled over.
7. Kicked the bucket.
8. Took the big hike.
9. Plotzed.
10. Kissed the floor.

Since most White deaths are from natural causes, and late in life to boot, the White person is generally afforded the luxury of time to prepare.

If the proper arrangements have been made, the funeral can go off like a well-oiled machine once the family has decided, for economic reasons, to pull the plug on Grandpa.

It is important to know the location of the family plot, the address of a reputable florist, and the going rates from your local Protestant minister. It is also important to check with the National Weather Service, since a thundershower can ruin even the nicest of funerals and frozen ground can spell double or even triple the cost of grave digging.

Let's say that everything is perfect: the sun is shining, the ground is soft, the flowers arrive, and the local TraveLodge had enough rooms for the bereaved from out of state. Now comes the "make it or break it" part of the service: the eulogy.

## THE EULOGY

There are only two rules for the eulogizer and they are cardinal:

1. Get the name of the deceased right.
2. Act as if you knew him.

After that, it's all poetic license coupled with a respect for how difficult it is for White people to stand for long periods of time.

It was extremely fortunate for us that during the writing of this book Jinx Harrison passed away. (You may recall him from earlier chapters.) It afforded us an opportunity to attend his funeral and tape the eulogy, which we here reproduce in its entirety.

The circumstances surrounding Jinx's last rites were not ideal. The rain never stopped, the flowers were late arriving, the ground was harder than Chinese arithmetic, and the TraveLodge was booked full with a U-Haul convention.

Still, undaunted, Rev. "Binky" Williams did his best to give the old geezer a great send-off.

Dearly beloved, we are gathered here at the
Pathways Memorial Cemetery and Driving
Range to pay our last respects to Edgar Phillip
Harrison. As you can see, it's raining cats and
dogs, which is exactly what "Jinx," as he came
to be called, would have hoped for. Why?
Because it brings the crappies right to the
surface, and Jinx loved to fish.

He was a fisherman, a simple fisherman, not
only in the gurgling streams of this great
country, but in the gurgling streams of life as
well. He put the worm of his knowledge on the
hook of his daring, and cast his line into the
raging seas of experience. Sure, there were
days when they just weren't biting and he went
home with an empty creel. So did our Christ.
But there were glorious days when he snagged
the small-mouth bass of truth. His bait was his

129

charm and his willingness to listen. His sinker was kidney stones and a love of fried foods. Unfortunately, it finally pulled him right off the boat, into the cattails of the Hereafter.

He was a veteran. A veteran of World War II. And as he himself was oft to say, "I didn't start this war, I simply helped it."

He was a kind and loving husband. As he once said to his late wife, Mabel, "You sweat less than any fat girl I ever danced with."

He was a strong and caring father. And I'm sure his children have many warm and moving stories to tell about "Dad."

I wish I personally knew more about the man Jinx Harrison. I wish I knew why he was called Jinx. To me he was just a mild-mannered Christian named Edgar who would show up every time we were raffling off an Oldsmobile down at the church. He never won one of those Oldsmobiles, but today he's won a bigger prize.

He's on his way to a place where an Oldsmobile can't help him.

He was a Rotarian, an Eagle Scout, and a longtime member of the Book-of-the-Month Club. And he spent many years of devoted service helping out the . . . you know, I can't really read this, the rain has completely washed away my scribbling here. That's a problem with a lot of these felt-tip markers. Suffice it to say, I wish I had known him and thank God there are those of you who did and are here today.

Let's just praise God and hope that he's in a better and drier place than we are. Amen.

It was beautiful, meaningful, and to the point. Afterward, the next of kin made a beeline to the lawyer's office for the reading of the last will and testament.

## THE LAST WILL & TESTAMENT OF
## EDGAR PHILLIP HARRISON

I, Edgar Phillip Harrison, being of sound mind and body, hereby bequeath the following stuff. A lot of the stuff I had planned on giving away or maybe selling before I died, but since I don't know when that will be, or was, then maybe I've already given it away or sold it. If you don't see it anywhere around the house, don't worry about it. I probably gave it away or sold it. It might be in the garage, I can't say for sure, it all depends on what it is.

There's always a load of stuff that finds its way out to the garage. Stuff that won't fit in your trunk when you're making a dump run. Plus, you hate like hell to throw something out that might be worth something. A lot of people collect old magazines, for instance, and so I bundled all of mine up with binder twine and set them in the basement by the water heater. If they're worth something, you're welcome to them. If not, throw them out. I was just afraid to lift them myself, with my back being so bad.

Most of you got all the upstairs stuff when Mabel died, so it's mostly just the junk in the basement, the junk in the garage, and my fishing gear, which I want to keep. This may sound selfish, but I don't know what's on the other side in the way of fishing and neither do you.

If for some godforsaken reason I should outlive all of you, then just cart it all off to the Goodwill with my blessing. (Not counting the fishing gear.) Otherwise, have at it.

Edgar Phillip Harrison

132

As you can see, having a legally binding last will and testament can take the guesswork and the backbiting out of inheritance. If you don't have a will, the loved ones you leave behind may have to stand around with their hands in their pockets while the court comes in and turns the family homestead that you busted your hump to pay off into a state-run "community center" where juvenile delinquents pee in the garden and spray dirty words on your wallpaper in Spanish.

The family homestead is something to be cherished and valued from generation to generation. It has a meaning beyond words for those left to carry on the family name. Of course if they have to widen the interstate, that's another story. That's progress. And they usually pay top dollar.

In conclusion, for those of you who find the whole subject of death, burial, and rotting to be morbid and depressing, cheer up. Death is simply a part of life. It's the last part. Let's face it, even Mamie Eisenhower finally died.

# 12
## Whither the White Man?

As we look around this great country of ours, we see many different and diverse groups of people. All of them, thanks to the freedom that America affords, are headed somewhere. For most of our non-Whites this means headed toward Whiteness. We see more and more Mexican-Americans with Polaroids. We see more and more Afro-Americans in Volvos. We see Japanese-Americans at McDonald's and Italian-Americans in Izod polo shirts. Soon the distinction of White-American may join the ranks of the dodo bird, the Edsel, and the non-Expand-A-Belt trouser. If others are headed toward Whiteness, where is the White man headed?

Certainly not backward, tempting and easy as that might be. It is impossible to picture the Whitey of the future with a bone through his nose savoring uncooked possum. Hopefully, since the only alternative is forward, there are still unexplored frontiers of Whiteness. Perhaps there is still room to move.

After a great deal of thinking, and literally hours of research, it seems to us that many of today's White Americans are in fact "off-White." Just like the color you chose for the kitchen cupboards. And why did you choose it? Because it doesn't show the dirt. It hides the dirt and still appears White to the naked eye and the potential home buyer.

The analogy is staggering.

For instance, is it possible for a man to be a part of White society and still, in the privacy of his own home, enjoy bagels and cream cheese? Yes. Is it possible for a White woman to tune in the local "soul" station and hum along with Marvin Gaye on the way to the dry cleaner's? Yes. Is it possible for White teenagers to reach voting age without ever having played badminton? Yes, yes, and more yes!

Of course, most Whites would never dream of taking risks like the above. They are happy just being plain White. But is there a Whiter Whiteness out there, still untouched? We believe there is. Before you start applauding us for our daring, it is not that original a thought. Actually we got it from a new, improved Fab commercial that advertised "Whiter Whites." Still, truth is truth, whether it's laundry or people.

In years to come, given the complexities and temptations of modern life, not to mention the lure of cheap Japanese goods, many Whites will become stitched into the patchwork quilt of multi-ethnic America. Indeed, it will become increasingly difficult for contemporary Whites to say no to German beer, French water, Swedish movies, and Mexican snack foods. On top of that, intermarriage will abound, and grandparents will be sending birthday cards to the likes of Jeanne-Marie Goldfarb and Ho Chi Minh Anderson.

The prize of pure Whiteness will go to those of great courage. The ones who know how to say, "No, thank you." Chinese food tonight? No, thank you. Free tickets to a Prince concert? No, thank you. Tapered shirts? No, thank you. It will take guts, but if priests can live without getting laid, it *can* be done.

We have a dream. We dream that as the year 2000 rolls around, the best of White culture will remain and that whole families, wearing only Expand-A-Belt

137

fashions, will still cook outdoors and make sweaters for their dogs without being branded social outcasts for doing so. Perhaps, in such a world, we may find another Norman Rockwell. We may find another Betty Crocker. We may find another J. C. Penney.

To some the future is there for the taking. For the White man, it is there for those who ask politely, "May I have some future, please?" But it's there and we wish them all the best.

And what, you may ask, what's beyond the year 2000? Hopefully, it will be a lot like *Star Trek*.

## THE WHITE MAN'S CREDO

I am a White person. My skin is White.
My family is White. My house is White.
My friends are White. My elected
officials are White. My teeth are as
White as I can get them. I like White.

I am open to other colors. I like my
lawn green. I like my juice orange.
I like my meat red. I like the
"purple mountain majesties" part of
"America the Beautiful."
I like the Cleveland Browns.

I believe that sex is for babies.
I may have said that wrong, but you
know what I mean.

I believe in keeping my opinions to
myself, if I ever have any. I believe
in fifty-five miles per hour, even in
Utah. I believe in the two-party
system. One on Friday, one on Saturday.
Just kidding. I believe in always
having an organized closet, never
swimming without a "buddy," and every
drop of rain that falls.

I cherish my Whiteness and will defend

it at all cost. I will defend it

against uncensored movies on cable

television. I will defend it against

the din of deafening popular music

trends. I will hold steadfast in the

face of inevitable Communist take-over.

I shall do everything in my power to

preserve and promote the way of life

that I think I sort of understand.

I shall stay White until I turn blue.

# APPENDIX
## Further Readings in White Culture

If you enjoyed this book and now feel, as many do, that it's about time you boned up on the White experience, then you probably need some educational guidance. After all, few of our major universities have White Studies departments and even fewer offer extension classes in "How to Be a White Person" for busy housewives and senior citizens. About the best you can do is go to a Toyota sales meeting in Japan where they're talking about how to capture the Iowa market, but they're all shouting at each other in Japanese, a language you probably don't understand.

The following reading list is the best we can do for now. Some of these books are third-grade material, if you prefer your reading material with pictures, and some are written by overeducated scholars who could turn out an incomprehensible twenty-page essay on how to get to the Safeway.

Let's face it, there's not a lot of good stuff on Whites out there. If there were, we wouldn't have written this tome. Like good White people, we saw a need and exploited it.

## SELECTED READINGS

"Harriet, Where Are My Pajamas!!!" a critical study of psychosexuality in the life of Ozzie Nelson. McDonald, Bernard P., Ph.D. University of Buffalo Press, New York, 1977.

"Entertaining with Spam," 1001 meat-flavored party ideas, with illustrations. Brown, Joyce Kendall. Tupperware Press, Wheaton, Illinois, 1969.

"If You've Met One, You Really Have Met Them All," the heartwarming story of a Jewish girl from New York raised by a plumbing contractor and his wife in western Kansas. Morgenstern-Jones, Judi. G. P. Putnam's Sons, New York, 1980.

"White Ways, Byways, and Overnight Accommodations," subtitled "The Whole White Journey Through Life in Easy-to-Read Road Map Form." Midwest AAA Publications, free to members on vacation, Kansas City, 1955.

"Ample Parking," the inspiring life story of shopping-mall mogul Harry "Sprawl" Adams. Adams, Harry. The Harry Adams Foundation Press, Kalamazoo, Michigan, 1968.

"I Can't Dance and No One Else Likes Stamp Collecting," White teenagers in crisis. Coleman, Robert W., M.D. University of Chicago Press, 1984.

"Why Did They Call Him Jinx?" one man's lifelong search for his World War II foxhole buddy. Bacon, Waldo. V.A. Publications, Washington, D.C., 1985.

"It's the New Testament, Charlie Brown, Not the Old One!" an illustrated version of the Bible starring Snoopy and the whole gang. Schulz, Charles. Ding-Dong Press, 1978.